Adventure in
Istanbul

THE SPY WHO WASN'T THERE ①

Adventure in
Istanbul

CORA TAYLOR

COTEAU BOOKS
WWW.COTEAUBOOKS.COM

Edited by Geoffrey Ursell.
Cover image, "Blue Mosque During Sunset" by Masterfile.
Models photographed by Austring Photography Ltd.
Cover montage and design by Duncan Campbell.
Book design by Karen Steadman.
Printed and bound in Canada by Marquis Bookprinting Inc.

National Library of Canada Cataloguing in Publication Data

Taylor, Cora, 1936-
Adventure in Istanbul / Cora Taylor

(The spy who wasn't there ; 1)
ISBN 1-55050-315-4

I. Title. II. Series: Taylor, Cora, 1936- . Spy who wasn't there ; 1.

PS8589.A883A64 2005   jC813'.54   C2005-902573-5

10 9 8 7 6 5 4 3 2 1

COTEAU BOOKS
401-2206 Dewdney Ave
Regina, Saskatchewan
Canada S4R 1H3

available in Canada and the US from:
Fitzhenry & Whiteside
195 Allstate Parkway
Markham, Ontario
Canada L3R 4T8

The publisher gratefully acknowledges the financial assistance of the Saskatchewan Arts Board, the Canada Council for the Arts, the Government of Canada through the Book Publishing Industry Development Program (BPIDP), and the City of Regina Arts Commission, for its publishing program.

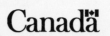

For my Grandson, Samuel Elwin Thomas,
who wanted a book about a boy named Sam
who was a detective. Sorry it took so long!

PART 1

VANISHING ACT

Candles flickered in the darkened room, making strange shadows cross the girl's face. Her voice, hesitant at first, became stronger as she read. She no longer fumbled with the strange pronunciation, but as her voice strengthened she became more comfortable with the words, until she spoke the final ones in a voice that no longer sounded like her own.

She stood for a moment in the eerie half-light, still holding the book. And then she began to disappear. Only when she heard the scream did she realize her sister had entered the room.

"I told Jennifer she shouldn't do it." Maggie picked absently at the cuff of her sweater. She spent half her time trying to keep her twin sister out of trouble and the other half covering for her.

"Do what? Disappear?" Her mother's voice had an unpleasant edge.

Maggie tugged at a bit of loose wool. She could imagine the reaction if she told the truth just now – Yes Mum, I told her not to disappear but she did it anyway!

Actually, what she'd told Jennifer was not to mess around with that old Magic book. Jen had found it at the University Library while their mother was looking up information for an essay. *The Black Book: Witchcraft, Black Magick and Alchemy*. Jennifer couldn't wait to get it home and try a few of the spells.

Smuggling it out of the library hadn't been a problem. Maggie never failed to admire Jennifer's genius for planning, even though it always came with a sinking feeling – here we go again.... Trouble.

"Go get a coffee at SUB and relax, Mum, just give us your library card and we'll check out your books. Practice for when we're students here...." This was accompanied by an angelic smile. Their mother went. At the car, Jennifer shocked Maggie by volunteering to sit in the back seat. Then Maggie realized she'd done it so that she could transfer the book from the briefcase to a backpack. Maggie's backpack, of course.

"Margaret! I want an explanation, and I want it now! And stop unravelling that sweater!"

This is it, Maggie thought. I'll just have to explain everything and get it over with. Except who'll believe me? She stared at the cuff of her sweater, or what was left of it. A large part of it was nothing more than squiggly yarn in her hand. She raised her eyes to her mother's left shoulder; she couldn't bear to look her in the eye. What I need now is a miracle, she thought desperately.

"I'm waiting, Margaret, and never mind making googly eyes."

Maggie couldn't help it. She was staring at the orange vase which had floated off the shelf behind her mother and was now drifting out into the middle of the room. It hovered for a moment before slamming to the floor with a crash.

"Now how did...?" Her mother turned angrily. "You stay right there, young lady, and think about what you are going to tell me when I get back with the dustpan." She stuck her head back around the doorway. "And I mean everything!"

"Okay, Maggie." Jennifer's voice threatened. "You talk and I am in a position to make your life very miserable!"

Maggie didn't like the tone of voice or the poke in the arm for emphasis. In fact, she didn't like anything about this situation.

She'd had the sinking feeling to end all sinking feelings when she'd walked into their bedroom that afternoon and found Jennifer in the flickering candlelight. Her voice sounded hollow, not like her at all. It made Maggie's skin crawl. She couldn't help but scream as Jennifer slowly began to vanish.

Then she heard Jen's triumphant, "It works! The spell works! I'm invisible!" Maggie felt herself being pounded on the back and grabbed to be swung around the room doing a victory dance with a sister she couldn't see.

This has got to be the lowest point in my life, Maggie had thought then, and I've had a lot of low points – all caused by Jennifer. She'd listened as Jennifer gloated, "Can you imagine what a terrific asset this will be when Sam and I set up our Detective Agency?"

Sam was their friend next door. He and Jennifer had been solving imaginary cases (and getting into trouble) since they were little kids. They seriously intended to have a detective agency when they grew up. They were going to let Maggie work in their office, answering the phone and doing the filing. Very generous. Maggie had other plans; she was going to study languages and be a diplomat.

Now, standing next to her invisible twin and waiting for her mother to come back from the kitchen, Maggie knew that the events of that afternoon hadn't been the lowest point in her life at all. That was yet to come. "I have to tell Mum *something!* she mumbled between clenched teeth.

"Don't do it, Maggie. Just give me time to get the wrinkles ironed out."

"Yeah, like the fact that the book doesn't have a spell to make an invisible person visible again?"

"Details, details.... Now you tell Mum that I've gone over to Sam's because we got stuck in the same group in Science. Tell her...tell her we went to the library to look something up."

When her mother came back, Maggie watched miserably as she picked up the pieces of the shattered vase. Why do I always get stuck making alibis for Jennifer? Probably something to do with being the eldest twin. She sighed. It wasn't fair being the responsible one. Being born eight minutes earlier shouldn't ruin your life like this. Jennifer probably won't be a detective when she grows up, Maggie thought grimly, she'll be an international jewel thief and *I'll* be the one who ends up in jail. She felt her breath catch. It came out somewhere between a sob and a sigh. "I'm sorry about the vase, Mum."

Her mother finished picking up the pieces, "Never mind. It was one of those presents you don't like very much but can't get rid of. Anyway, it wasn't your fault." Her voice softened. "And I know that whatever Jennifer is up to isn't your fault either. That is, if she is up to something. But you have to understand, dear, that a mother is bound to be upset when her daughter disappears. So, if you do know where she is, say so!"

Maggie felt a sharp poke in her back and began to explain about the fictitious science project. She had just got to the library part, when the doorbell rang.

"I'll dump the broken glass in the garbage," she offered, making her escape.

She was in the kitchen when her arm was grabbed and nearly pulled from its socket. She was being yanked towards the front door as Jennifer hissed in her ear. "It's Sam. Quick, don't let him say anything!"

She allowed herself to be hauled into the front hallway. Her arms were waving – being waved – in some crazy signal. Sam just stared.

"Hi Sam, are you and Jennifer back from the library already?" Play along, she mouthed at him silently. "I'll bet Jennifer sent you for my science text. She forgot to take it with her."

"What's...?" began Sam. Maggie could see his lips pressed against his teeth as if an invisible hand had been clamped over his mouth. His eyes widened in horror. Luckily her mother wasn't facing him anymore.

"All right," she sighed. "Whatever is up, and I'm not buying the science project for a minute, I suppose it's just another of Jennifer's hare-brained schemes. I've got to go back to campus and get a book I need. I won't be more than half an hour," she said, glancing at her watch. "And I expect to see Jennifer here when I get back!" She left, mumbling to herself, "The girl never says a word to me – just disappears. Vanishes. I don't like it."

Poor Mum. Maggie wondered if her mother's anger went deeper. People disappearing on her – first her husband and now her daughter.

S am had to admit this was a new one, even for Jennifer. He was used to her wild schemes – he'd participated in most of them. Ever since the time when they were four and she'd tied umbrellas to their arms and persuaded him that they could jump off the garden shed, though, he'd been a bit more suspicious of anything that involved him. That time he'd ended up with a broken leg. Jennifer had somehow escaped unscathed. Landing on top of him had broken her fall.

This time, even after the initial confusion of Maggie's wild signalling and then the feeling of Jennifer's hand over his mouth, he hadn't been all that surprised. You never knew what would happen at the Arnold house. He hadn't realized Jennifer was invisible at that point, not until he'd turned around to get even. Then he'd been so shocked he'd barely heard any of the story Maggie was concocting about science projects and borrowing books.

Now he was sitting on Jennifer's bed, trying to get the details. It was a bit disconcerting directing questions into thin air.

"If that spell from the book made you invisible, maybe there's a spell to undo it." He spoke toward the window, where he'd last heard Jennifer's voice. The answer came from behind him, causing him to jerk his head around. I'll have whiplash if she keeps this up, Sam thought.

"I looked," said Jennifer's voice. Now the book on the dresser was rising into the air, opening and drifting toward them as pages turned. Maggie stared for a minute. Then, giving a shudder, she snatched the book and began to look through the index.

"There are spells in here for just about anything," she said, reading out loud, "Earthquake, eternal youth, health, love, plague: cure or inflict..."

"You missed the invisibility one," Sam interrupted. "*I*. It would come between 'health' and 'love.'"

Maggie sounded desperate. "That's just it, Sam, the spell that Jen used isn't listed with the rest. It...it was on a funny old piece of paper, sort of stuck in the book."

The old paper crackled as it floated over to Sam.

"*...mortale perficiat qua hoc opus ut invisibiliter ire posim,*" he read aloud. "Wow! How did you get this spell to work? I can't even pronounce the words...*et hoc experimentum me invisibilem faciat...*"

Maggie snatched the paper away from him. "Sam! Stop it! We don't need two invisible people around here."

"Calm down, Maggie," Jennifer's voice came from right beside her, "he only read the last bit. You probably need the whole spell. And...and I guess pronunciation doesn't matter. You sort of get into it, then it kind of takes over and gets easier as you go along."

"Well, we've got less than half an hour before Mum gets

back and has a nervous breakdown. Really, Jennifer, you are a great big pain of a sister, you know that. I'm always in the soup on account of you. You drive me crazy!" Maggie sounded as if she was on the verge of tears. She was staring at her sweater sleeve which was unravelled almost to the elbow. "Now look at what you made me do!"

"Who cares about your stupid sweater! This is an emergency!"

Sam stood up. "I hate to interrupt this sisterly bonding ritual but we do have a problem to solve." He wasn't used to hearing desperation in Jennifer's voice. Maggie wasn't the only one who was losing it.

Maggie took two steps and collided with Jennifer. "At least do something so we don't bump into you!"

A pillow rose from the bed, collapsed around the middle and went jerkily back and forth. "There, now you can see where I am."

Sam thought for a bit. "I suppose that *is* the important part...seeing where you are, that is. It's not as if you don't exist anymore...you're there, we just can't see you. Maybe," he said to Maggie, "we could spray paint her. Tell your mum it was the science project."

"Hmmm..." Maggie looked as if she was considering the idea seriously. "I suppose we could use paint remover afterwards. The spell might wear off eventually."

"No way, you two. It's a dumb idea. Besides, I could get lead poisoning or something, and die."

"Well," Sam was beginning to enjoy this, "at least Maggie and I wouldn't have any trouble disposing of the body...after we got the paint off!"

Maggie giggled and got a pillow in the face.

"Come on, you guys." Jennifer was beginning to sound desperate. "Think! Think! How would you reverse a spell?"

"Kiss a frog?" Maggie hid behind the pillow.

"That's it!" Sam felt triumphant. "Reverse the spell. Get it?"

He could tell by the look on her face that Maggie didn't get it at all. He was about to explain but suddenly he was being pounded on the back, grabbed by the shoulders and yanked to his feet. Now he was being hauled around in circles, dancing with an invisible partner. It must look pretty stupid, he thought. He got a glimpse of Maggie's face, an interesting combination of confusion and horror, but he didn't have much chance to analyze it just now, he was too busy trying not to trip over Jennifer's invisible feet.

JENNIFER 3

Jennifer let go of Sam and watched him collide with Maggie. She felt better than she had since the whole thing started. Actually, she felt fine being invisible. Light. Airy. Probably had better posture than she'd had in her whole life. But there were complications. How do you explain something like this to your mother – or anyone else for that matter? If Maggie hadn't come along and caught her in the act of disappearing, she'd never have believed it either. Then Jennifer would never have been able to get her to help out, and she had to admit that she needed Maggie. For all that it was tough having a perfect-student, neat-and-tidy sister – Maggie had her good points. People believed just about anything she said, so all Jennifer had to do was persuade her to say things Jennifer's way. Even then, because Maggie was Maggie, if people didn't believe her, they forgave her because they assumed it was Jennifer's doing. Case in point: the science project story and their mother's reaction to it.

Still, she was exuberant as she danced Sam around the room. Invisibility was great but she'd have to learn how to control it.

"That's it! Sam, you're a genius! I'll say the spell backwards!" She stopped suddenly serious. "I hope just reversing the order of the words is all I need. It's hard enough to say those words forwards."

"Come on, Maggie, help me set things up the way I had them before. Light the candles. Sam, turn out the light."

Jennifer had to admit that Maggie did a good job. Her orderly mind had obviously held onto the picture of what the room looked like when she'd come in. Jennifer held the book. The sheet of paper was lying between its opened pages just as it was before. Carefully, she began to intone the words.

"Faciat invisibilem me experimentum hoc et posim...." Reading backwards wasn't that hard. The words didn't make any sense to her either way. "...Mistletan, Picea, Quercus, Ulmus, Acer....

She concentrated on the strange words. It was just as she'd told Sam, even reading them backwards, they were developing a rhythm that pulled her along.

"...*Fraxinus, Betula, Salix, Lonicera!*" she finished triumphantly.

There was complete silence in the room. Nobody moved. Jennifer didn't dare look up. She just kept staring at the paper in the book. Staring down at where her hand should be. Then she heard it. The sound of a car on the gravel in the back lane, her mother's car pulling into the parking spot. Then the motor died and the car door slammed.

Jennifer let out a long low sigh and looked up. Sam sat motionless staring at her.

Maggie looked as if she was going to cry. "It's not going to work," she said, her voice trembling.

They heard the back door open and close and their mother moving around in the kitchen below.

Maggie moved at last, shifting nervously. "What will we do?"

What could they do? It was too late for the spray paint idea. Crazy as it was it was the sort of thing she would do. Her mother would be mad but just in the usual way. They'd just have to make up another alibi for her to still be at Sam's. Or she could lock herself in the bathroom, pretend to be taking a bath, but then what? She'd have to come out eventually. Would the spell wear off by itself?

"Look," breathed Sam, "here she comes!"

Jennifer stared at the door expecting her mother to walk through it though she hadn't heard her climbing the stairs. Then she realized that Sam wasn't talking about her mother. He and Maggie were both looking at her, their eyes wide. Her hands and feet began to tingle. That "needles and pins" feeling you got if you'd been sitting too long on one leg. She looked down.

It was true. There was a fuzzy outline of fingers as the hand holding the paper began to show.

Maggie stared in amazement and relief. It was happening. Jennifer was starting to reappear. First, foggy shapes that were her hands and feet, then her nose and ears. Those gradually became solid as new parts started to form. That was how it had worked before. Maggie had noticed Jennifer's hands disappearing just after she finished reading the spell. Misty arms and legs began to connect to Jennifer's hands and feet. There was no body, just unattached arms and legs as Jennifer's hands waved over her head in a victory salute.

When they heard their mother's footsteps coming up the stairs Jennifer was almost complete. She had a body and hair, but her head hadn't quite formed yet. There was a nose and lips, but no face. Jennifer stared at the door. Then, a knock.

"Jennifer!"

"Yes, Mum?" Jennifer's faceless lips moved eerily.

"I will talk to you after supper, young lady!"

Maggie held her breath, watching the doorknob turn. She glanced back at Jen. Just in time, her sister's face filled in as the door opened.

"I picked up some pizza, come and get it while it's hot!" Mrs. Arnold looked around the room. "And turn the light on, the candlelight makes you look as though you've all seen a ghost!"

Sam stayed for supper. It was a fairly silent meal. Even Jennifer seemed thoughtful for a change.

Finally Mrs. Arnold broke the awkward silence. "So what's this famous 'science project' you two are cooking up?"

Maggie felt quietly smug. Let them weasel out of that one. She sat back looking at Jennifer expectantly, trying not to smile too broadly.

"And, just when is it due?" Mrs. Arnold continued, "I didn't hear anything about it before." She turned to Maggie, "What about you Margaret, I haven't heard you talking about anything like that."

Why, oh why, Maggie wondered, when it was Jennifer who was supposed to be questioned, did *she* end up being the one who had to answer first? Now she would be buying time for Jennifer to make up an answer whether she wanted to or not. She took her time about swallowing her last bite of pizza. "Oh, I'm not doing a project. I'm doing an essay on the various space shuttles, from Sputnik on." She looked at her mother. It was true. It was totally true. They'd been assigned essays, not projects. "And it's due next Wednesday."

"Yes," said Jennifer, nodding innocently. "You had a choice, Sam and I were going to do a project. Something to do with candlepower...." She looked to Sam for help. Jennifer was hopeless in Science. Maggie knew she'd begun with the topic of tuberous vegetables and her essay so far had been mostly taken from the encyclopaedia and the *Amazing Potato Book*.

Sam came through for her as usual. "Actually, we'd thought we might do a comparison on Candlepower and Electricity...the ratio of light and heat...." He looked politely at Mrs. Arnold. "Does anyone want that last piece of double cheese pizza?"

Later, lying on her bed in the room she shared with Jennifer, Maggie listened drowsily as Sam and Jennifer sat on the floor playing Scrabble and arguing about how they would use the invisibility. Sam wanted to wait. Keep it exclusively for use in the Great Detective Agency. Jennifer thought they should experiment with it, make sure it was completely under control. And in the meantime, there were certain people she had plans for.

"Can you imagine the look on Ashley Beneton's face, if suddenly when she's trying to impress Jason Paulus, a strand of that oh-so-perfectly-blonde hair of hers goes across her upper lip like a moustache? Or she trips on something that isn't there and falls flat on those false eyelashes of hers? Or..."

"Her eyelashes aren't false," interrupted Maggie. "She just happens to be one of those incredibly lucky people who have blonde hair and long black eyelashes. It's one of the injustices of the world that you'll have to learn to live with."

"Not anymore," Jennifer gloated. "Now, I can get some revenge – invisible revenge."

"Not practical," Sam pointed out, "we can actually *do* something worthwhile with this. Solve major cases someday. I mean we could follow anybody anywhere. Think of it!"

"*I* could follow anybody anywhere, you mean." Jennifer said smugly. "We don't know if it will work on you."

Maggie watched as Jennifer preened herself. She tossed her head, an affectation she had copied from Ashley. Except it worked much better with Ashley's blonde mane. Jennifer's long brown hair with its tight, thick curls barely moved. Maggie made a point of telling Jen each time she did it that she'd give herself whiplash someday. Jennifer's hair bugged Maggie anyway. They'd agreed when they started Junior High that they'd adopt different hairstyles. Being identical twins was enough of a hassle without having people mix them up. That had been alright when they started, Maggie had kept her hair short, the curls tight to her head. A good cut and she didn't have to do anything to it. But when she'd suggested to Jen that *she'd* like to have the long hair for a change, Jen had refused point-blank. So now Maggie was stuck with the boring short style and she was sick of it. She decided not to say anything – she hoped Jen *would* get whiplash.

"What do you mean it won't work for me?" Sam was indignant. "Why shouldn't it work for me? If I hold the spell and say the words, of course it will work for me. What I'm worried about is: what if there's a limit to it... I mean what if you can only use it a certain number of times? Like three wishes, for instance."

Jennifer looked dismayed. "I hadn't thought of that."

"Trouble is..." Sam pointed out, "...the only way to find out is to use it two more times...and then if *is* three, it will be too late."

Jennifer poked sadly at the Scrabble squares. "You're right. Ashley Beneton's life is spared my vengeance...for now." She arranged the letters g-l-y-p-h on the board to follow Sam's word *petrol*.

Maggie leaned over the edge of the bed to get a better look. "What, may I ask, is a 'petrolglyph,' Jennifer?"

Jennifer moved around so that her back blocked Maggie's view. "You know," she said impatiently, "those drawings we saw by the Milk River, last summer...at Writing-on-Stone National Park?"

"That's *petro*glyph..." Maggie corrected..

"Butt out, Muggins!" Jennifer snapped, "isn't it past your bedtime?"

"What we need," said Sam ignoring them, "is a mystery. Something legitimate to solve. Then it will be alright to use the spell. It wouldn't even have to be big stuff – a little mystery would do."

Maggie rolled over to face the wall. She was sleepy. But she couldn't help smiling to herself. They'd have their mystery alright. And no doubt things would be tough for awhile when they found out the spell was missing.

It had been easy enough. She'd stayed behind a minute to change her sweater before going downstairs for supper. Even the Great Detectives would have trouble finding it taped behind a picture in Mum's room.

She'd supposed she should have torn it up and flushed it down the toilet or burned it or something, but there hadn't been time. Anyway, it just might come in handy some day....and it wasn't often she got to put one over on Jennifer. Her smile broadened. It was a lovely feeling.

JENNIFER 5

Tuesday evening Jennifer sat at the desk in their room. She was staring at the wall, feeling a bit queasy. In fact, when their mother had asked at supper if they wanted to go to a show with her, Maggie had accepted and Jennifer had surprised them and said no. Her Science paper was due tomorrow and she was feeling guilty because she hadn't worked on it, even though she'd told her mother she was almost finished. She was back to the potatoes. Besides, she just didn't feel as if she had the energy to go anywhere. She shuffled the pages of notes she'd made and stared at her opening paragraph. Ugh.

She could hear her mother and Maggie getting ready to leave. Maggie, of course, had finished her paper and rewritten it twice. Jennifer flopped her head onto the desk. If there'd been anyone there she'd have banged it a few times for a laugh, but alone there was not much point and besides, she didn't need a headache, too. She waited, listening for the sound of the front door. Instead she heard her mother's steps on the stairs. Probably coming to give me one last chance to go. Jennifer had not been exactly accurate about what she had left to do on the essay. "Just have to make a clean copy," had been the way she'd explained it at supper.

But her mother wasn't coming to invite her to the show. She looked worried, even distraught, Jennifer thought.

"Jennifer! Have you seen my watch? I thought I'd left it in the bathroom...kept forgetting it, but I wasn't concerned because I was sure that's where it was. Now, I wonder if the strap broke or something...." She stared around the room, as though she expected to see it hanging from the wall.

"It's just that I don't remember having it since the weekend, there's no telling..." her voice trailed off.

Jennifer was surprised. "Hey Mum, don't worry! It'll probably show up. Maybe it fell off in the car, in the trunk when you were lifting out groceries, or somewhere in the house, when you were making beds, there's hundreds of places..." Jennifer stopped. *That* was not the right approach. "Anyway," she said trying to be more cheerful. "It was pretty old – out of style, you could get one of those neat Swatches or something."

To Jennifer's amazement there were tears in her mother's eyes as she turned towards the door. When she spoke it was so softly Jennifer could barely hear her. "It was a present."

Jennifer's hands gripped the desk. "From Dad?" she breathed. But her mother was gone and the door clicked shut behind her.

Jennifer stared at the door. She should have known better. Her mother had refused to talk about their father since the divorce. That was when he'd quit flying for Air Canada and gone to fly in the Middle East. She and Maggie had found out about the divorce from Grandma Gagnon. And that was when? Three years ago, shortly after their tenth birthday.

She got up from the desk and walked over to the bed. Slowly she knelt and slid her hand between the mattress and the box spring. It took nearly her whole arm's reach before her fingers touched the flat leather case. One her grandfather had brought back from a meeting and everyone thought Jennifer had carelessly lost. Slowly she worked it back towards her.

Sitting cross-legged on the floor by the bed, she carefully undid the flap. There wasn't much inside, but it was all she had of her father. There was a snapshot of him in his Air Canada pilot's uniform. That seemed such a long time ago. She'd Scotch-taped it together after she found it in the wastepaper basket around the time she found out about the divorce. There were three other pictures. Her favourite was one of him pushing her on a swing. She'd have been about five. She still remembered that day and the feeling of his hands, gripping her waist so that when he pushed her she wouldn't slide forward on the seat, and then he'd let go and she could feel the wind in her face. She closed her eyes, remembering. It had been a beautiful day. Even now she could almost taste the sunshine and feel the bubble of happiness inside.

She opened her eyes. The picture captured all that. The look of joy on her face. But what she loved most about the picture was the look on his face. Until the photo was developed she hadn't realized that his look mirrored hers – so alive, so happy to be alive.

And where was he now? She didn't even know if he was alive. As far as their mother was concerned it didn't seem to matter. In the three years that had passed since the divorce he might as well have been dead.

Did Maggie feel that way too? Maybe. Jennifer didn't know. Maggie did her work, studied, tried to keep Jennifer out of trouble as much as she could, and kept her feelings pretty much to herself. At least her feelings about their father.

At first they hadn't said anything because everything they said, every question, upset their mother. And they hadn't talked much between themselves because it always ended up in a fight. Maggie calm and cool, Jennifer in a rage of tears. At least they'd known enough not to do it when Mum was at home.

Maggie seemed to think that the divorce didn't make much difference. They had not seen their father in the year before. Their mother had decided to take some time off from teaching and go back to university. It was her excuse to sell the house and move closer to campus. Jennifer was sure it was because she did not want anything to remind her of their father – like the torn pictures in the wastepaper basket. Luckily Grampa Gagnon had persuaded Mum to stay. "It's enough...the divorce is enough..." he'd said, "let the girls have their home." So they stayed but any reminders of their father – pictures, ornaments, even the porch furniture he'd built – had been replaced.

So why had she kept the watch? Jennifer wasn't even sure it was from her father, only that her mother had worn it for as long as she could remember. She wished Maggie was home. Maybe she'd remember where the watch had come from. Maybe Mum would have told her.

"Maybe, Jennifer Arnold," she said to herself out loud, "maybe you'd just better stop worrying about it and get that stupid paper written!" She sighed and put the pictures carefully back in the leather folder and slid them under the mattress.

She'd phone Sam first though, let him know about the watch. Maybe that could be their mystery. She pulled the phone down from the bedside table and lay on the floor as she talked. At least she could postpone the essay a little longer.

She felt dizzy when she stood up. As if she'd been sitting too long and stood up too quickly. Or, she thought to herself hopefully, as if she was coming down with something. She let herself hope a bit longer. She'd be sick tomorrow. No point in doing the essay if she wasn't going to be in school to hand it in, was there? The trouble with being a twin was that didn't work. Maggie would be going to school. Their mother would insist that Maggie hand in Jennifer's paper. Otherwise, unless she could manage to be in a coma tomorrow, she would have to spend her day in bed writing about potatoes.

She sighed and crossed the room and plopped down in front of the desk. She began with the material she'd copied out of the *World Book:* "A tuber is the thick, enlarged part of a stem that grows underground. The potato is the best example of the tuber." She changed that to: "The potato is the most common example of a tuber, which is the thick, lumpy part of a stem that grows underground." It wasn't *exactly* copying, she consoled herself. It also wasn't going to get her a very good mark.

It was nearly 9:30 when she finished. Mum and Maggie would be home soon. Jennifer reached for the switch on the desk lamp. She was still feeling funny. Not sick anymore, just not right. Strange. The light clicked off and she sat a minute before she realized what was wrong. She'd reached for the switch, felt it, clicked it, but just before the light went off she hadn't seen her hand. She turned on the light again. Definitely no hand. Strange, it was there a minute ago when she was writing. Had she become invisible again? It can't be, she thought, I haven't done the spell, haven't touched it, haven't even looked at it. Not since Sunday. She dashed to the mirror. All she could see were the beds and the pictures on the wall behind her.

"Don't panic, Jennifer," she spoke calmly, carefully to the place in the mirror where her face should be. "Do *not* panic!"

Thank goodness the *Black Book* was still in the desk drawer. One more day and it would have to be returned or her mother would get a notice about it. Of course she'd keep the paper with the spell on it. She flipped through the pages, expecting to find the thin old parchment. It wasn't there. She held the book by the spine, shaking it, hoping against hope that the paper would flutter out. Nothing. Now she *was* panicking. Frantically she searched the drawer the book had been in. It *had* to be there, she'd closed the book with it inside. She'd held the book while her mother looked in, and then before they went down for pizza had placed it in this same drawer. The book was still here, but the paper with the spell on it was gone. How? It couldn't walk away, or could it? It was magic, but – and then she knew. Maggie. Maggie had somehow removed it.

Jennifer clenched her fists. "When I get my hands on you Muggins, you're dead meat." I don't even know if it will work but it's the only hope, Jennifer thought. "Don't panic, Jennifer!" She moved around turning out the lights. Just in time, too, because she heard the car drive in, saw the lights shining on the wall behind her. She did the only thing she could think of – climbed quickly into bed. Yes, her head made a dent in the pillow, the blankets made a reassuring hump. It would look like she was there. She pulled the sheet up so that it would cover her hair. Luckily her bed was furthest from the door.

"Jennifer?" She heard her mother's voice as the door opened. "Jennifer!"

"**D**on't tell me your sister's already asleep?" Maggie slipped in the door past her mother. It certainly looked that way. There was a sleepy mumble from Jennifer's bed but she didn't move.

"Alright Dear, see you in the morning!"

"Goodnight Mum...and thanks for the show," Maggie whispered.

She undressed quickly and slipped into bed. Her mother would be going to bed early too, she had an early class. The thin line of light under the door vanished as the hall light went out. Maggie lay there remembering bits of the movie, almost asleep. Whack! She was being shaken and thumped on the back – hard.

"Where is it, Maggie you scumbag," Jennifer's voice hissed in her ear. Another thump, even harder.

Maggie was about to howl in protest when a hand clamped over her mouth, and all she could manage was a muffled growl as her lips were smashed against her teeth. She felt Jennifer sitting on top of her chest, her voice coming from directly above.

"I said," Jennifer sounded furious, "where...is...it?"

The words were emphasized as Jennifer bounced on her knocking her breath out. Whatever *it* was, Maggie thought, she'd certainly never seen Jennifer this upset. She opened her eyes and tried to squirm free. It took a moment in the dim light but there was definitely nobody sitting on her. She couldn't see Jennifer but she could certainly feel the weight of her. The hand came off her mouth and the bedside light was switched on. Nobody there. Except, of course, there was. Jennifer was jumping on her again.

"Oh...my...!" Maggie gasped for breath. "Jennifer... you...got...invisible...again!" She struggled to heave Jennifer off of her. "Ooof! Jen...Get...Off...Ooof!"

Jennifer's feet thumped to the floor and Maggie lay wheezing, trying to fill her aching chest. She spoke as soon as she had the breath. "Jennifer, don't you realize how stupid it is to mess with that spell?" Maggie's breath was back now and she was working up to be furious. How dare Jennifer start jumping on her in the middle of the night. And how dare she complicate things by playing with spells and getting invisible again. Hadn't they had enough trouble with it the last time? That's why she'd hidden the stupid spell – Maggie stopped, puzzled.

"You found the spell?" She wasn't mad now, just amazed and curious. She saw the pillow on Jennifer's bed rising up in time to lift her arms to defend herself before it landed with a thwack on her head.

"Found it...?" Thwack! The pillow rose and fell for emphasis. "I...didn't find it!" Thwack! "If I had found it..." Thwack! "I wouldn't still be invisible, would I!" Jennifer's voice rose to a sob, the pillow stopped and was hugged around the middle as Jennifer's bed heaved.

Maggie was incredulous. "So how did you get invisible in the first place?"

"It just ha-ha-happened!" Jennifer really was sobbing now. "And I couldn't find the spell to try to get back to normal before Mum got home because..." Jennifer's voice was changing back to the former fury "...because, *you'd* stolen it and hidden it!"

Maggie sat up, there was that sinking feeling again. "Oooh Jennifer! You didn't do anything and it just happened?"

"Nothing...No...thing! I felt a little queasy after supper...not too bad and then working on my paper I felt..." At this point Maggie was sure Jennifer shrugged or made a face, hard to tell, the pillow she was holding barely moved. "But then I always feel a little sick when I'm doing homework, you know...."

Maggie didn't know. She didn't mind doing homework all that much, especially if she knew what she was doing and was making progress. She had to take Jennifer's word that for her it was painful.

"Anyway," Jennifer continued, "it wasn't until I'd finished that I noticed I was invisible again. And then..." her voice turned hard again and Maggie was just as glad she couldn't see her face because Jennifer could give a look that would freeze your blood, "...then..." the pillow was rising in the air again. Maggie rolled aside quickly before it hit. It's hard to dodge an opponent you can't see, she decided.

"So!" Jennifer was behind her now with a choke hold, that tightened for emphasis with each word. "So...Where...Is...It!"

Maggie struggled to speak. "Let go..." she gasped. "I'll...tell..." She rubbed her throat. "You aren't going to like this..." she began apologetically, and then as it seemed Jennifer's arm was tightening again, hurried on, "I hid it in Mum's room."

"You what?" Jennifer let go, moved, and Maggie fell back against the bed. When she spoke next it was the tone of voice that went with the look that froze your blood. "*Where* in Mum's room, pray tell?"

"Behind the photo of you and I when we were seven." Maggie didn't have to add, "the one that was taken the day Dad gave us our first two-wheelers", she knew Jennifer would remember too. Actually Maggie always wondered why that was the birthday snapshot their mother had taken to be enlarged and framed, but then maybe she didn't make the same connection that the two of them did. Perhaps to her it was just a good picture. The bikes wouldn't have had as much significance to her.

Suddenly the door swung open. Maggie sat up and waited, her eyes on the doorway. Even though she expected it, it was startling to see the picture come floating across the room as the door closed again.

"Okay, you get it out." The picture was thrust into her hands. "I'd better put it back right away, or Mum'll notice it in the morning. It's easier to replace when I'm still invisible...if I *do* get visible again..." Jennifer's voice trailed off uncertainly.

Maggie pried at the backing, slipped it off, slid the carefully folded parchment out, and handed the picture to Jennifer. Folding the spell had not been a good idea. It cracked almost in two as she unfolded it. Maggie could hear

Jennifer moving around. She was lighting candles. Maggie thought of helping, then decided to stay put. It wouldn't do to bump Jennifer, she might knock over a candle and start a fire.

"Faciat invisibilem me..." Jennifer began softly.

She should know it by heart soon, Maggie thought and then wished she hadn't. She crossed her fingers and hoped that this time the spell would hold and Jennifer would have sense enough not to try it again. She crossed her arms and legs as well for good measure and waited.

Sam woke up to the whine of the garage door closing as his dad left for work. His alarm was set but he never waited for it, the garage door always did the trick.

Mornings in the Elwin house often made Sam think he lived alone. His mother never got up until long after he'd left for school. His dad left before he was awake. He used to feel sorry for himself but then he'd decided it was probably just as well. He wouldn't have any trouble leaving home and being on his own. At least not in the mornings.

He threw the bedspread across his rumpled bed, whacked the pillow a couple of times and was finished what passed for bed-making in his book. Had to hurry if he was supposed to be over at Jen's place before school.

He had just finished printing the last of his essay on the Fauna of the Galapagos Islands when she phoned last night. He'd been surprised to hear her voice. When the Arnold car left earlier in the evening with Maggie in the front seat he'd just assumed that Jennifer was out of sight in the back.

Obviously not. Wonder of wonders, she was home working on her essay, or about to work on it.

Sam thought about what she'd said. "The Mystery of the Missing Watch" didn't exactly send him into orbit. And, what is more, he thought as he brushed his teeth, it shouldn't have been very exciting to Jennifer either, for all that she'd tried to point out what Sherlock Holmes had managed to do with the "Case of the Purloined Letter." Jennifer would have been the first to scoff at anything so minor as finding a lost watch. So, Sam puzzled, there was obviously more to it. And that, he decided as he slipped into his Nikes, had more to do with her response when he'd asked for more details as to why Mrs. Arnold was so upset about losing it. She'd said it was a present and Jennifer, being Jennifer, had decided that meant it was from her father.

Sam could read the rest into it. He knew that Jennifer missed her father, more than she'd ever admit. Once Sam's Mum had said that Jennifer was a daredevil like her father, and Jennifer had positively beamed, even though Sam was sure that it hadn't been meant as a compliment. It was true that even though the Arnold twins looked so much alike, they were as different as two people could be. This was because, Sam's mother said, Maggie was the same steady sort that her mother was, while Jennifer took after her father. Sam could vouch for the fact that Jennifer wanted to be like her father. That business with the umbrellas and the shed roof had been because she wanted to be a pilot, too.

Sam remembered James Arnold best from when he was flying with Air Canada. He'd been on overseas flights, gone for days, sometimes weeks, at a time. Then he'd taken that job flying in Dubai and some of the other Arab Emirates and not long after that – well he hadn't come back. Sam remembered looking the places up on the map with Jennifer.

And how shocked Mr. Wendel, their Social teacher, had been when she knew where Baghdad was when they discussed the war in Iraq in class. But Sam was never sure which had come first, the divorce or the not coming back. It wasn't something he dared talk to Jennifer about. He'd guessed that James Arnold's taking the permanent overseas job had been sort of an official separation. Rita Arnold wasn't the type to talk about things like that, even to her daughters.

Now, Sam thought, as he grabbed his backpack and closed the front door behind him, maybe they'd get a chance to find out something, for Jennifer's sake. And they could do it in the guise of solving the Mystery of the Missing Watch.

To begin with, he thought, as he rang the doorbell, they could find out if there was an inscription. Gift watches sometimes had them. Obviously, they'd need it if they were going to put up Lost posters. Jennifer would like it especially if it was something from her Dad. She needed that sort of thing.

Maggie opened the door. "Hi Sam," she waved towards the stairs, "She's up there, late as always, see if you can speed her up." She turned towards the kitchen. "Will you have the usual?"

"Thanks Maggie," he said gratefully.

He was pretty good about breakfast on his own but it was nice sitting down with company. Maggie anyway – Jennifer was always racing around doing last-minute things.

The bedroom door was open. Maggie's bed was neatly made. Jen's side of the room looked like a disaster area waiting for the emergency relief team to arrive. The only neat spot on her side was the rows of hats she had arranged on the wall. Jennifer loved hats.

"I'm in the bathroom, Sam," came Jennifer's voice. "Talk to me!"

"Okay," he leaned his back against the door. "Here's the plan. We'll need a good description of the watch...brand name...type of strap...colour...you know, gold or silver...stuff like that. When we've got that I'll make some nice posters to shove in people's mailboxes around the neighbourhood." He wasn't going to give away the inscription bit, just yet. "We'll have to question your mother about her activities, exactly where she's been since she was last aware that she had it. We'll probably have to stick up some notices on bulletin boards at the university, maybe the neighbourhood mall and like that. We need..." he said, really getting into it, "...to know if your mum wants to offer a reward. We need..." He didn't get any further, the door behind him opened and he'd have fallen if Jennifer hadn't given him a mighty push, propelling him across the hall. He spun around to confront her.

"What the...," he began. "Jennifer! You've gone and used the spell again." He was furious. "I thought we agreed to save it. And don't try to pretend that the Mystery of the Missing Watch requires invisibility!"

"Control yourself!" A finger was poking into his chest.

"Breakfast!" Maggie called. "Get a move on Jen."

There was a thumping noise of Jennifer going downstairs. Then Maggie's voice shrieking and simultaneously a crash.

When he got to the kitchen, Maggie was standing white-faced staring at a spilled bowl of cereal which was being mopped up by a paper towel that seemed to magically move on its own.

For one crazy moment it occurred to Sam that Jennifer could probably get a job doing TV commercials.

Maggie continued to stare. "It happened again?"

"Right," came Jennifer's voice as a double handful of cereal and paper towel floated across the room to fall into the garbage.

"I started feeling funny again and then as I was brushing my teeth...they disappeared."

Maggie led the way up the stairs to the bedroom and started arranging the candles.

"Listen you two, you'd better hurry," the piece of parchment was being smoothed against the desk. "Get going. Mag, tell them I'm sick or something...I'll show up later...." Jennifer's laugh had a catch to it, "...if I show up at all!"

They started down the stairs and Jennifer's backpack sailed after them. "Hand in my paper for me...I actually got it done on time, might as well hand it in...." Her voice was muffled by the bedroom door closing.

"She's really done it this time." Maggie grabbed the pieces of looseleaf that had been crammed into Jennifer's backpack, smoothed the pages flat, found a spare paperclip in the pocket of her own backpack and placed Jennifer's paper neatly beside her own. Sam noticed that Maggie's paper was enclosed in one of those clear plastic folders. It figured.

"Why?" Sam followed her down the steps. "Why, on earth...?"

Maggie stopped so suddenly he ran into her. "Why?" She faced him and her expression was more than just worried. It gave Sam a nervous feeling. A very nervous feeling. "I don't know why it's happening...Jennifer's not using the spell to become invisible. It...it just happens. This is the second time. Last night when I got home from the movie she was invisible, but reversing the spell brought her back. Now it's happened again."

"I thought that the invisibility might wear off after a while..." he said thoughtfully, "it never occurred to me that the *visibility* would." In spite of the warm spring day, Sam shivered. What if reversing the spell didn't work one of these times?

JENNIFER ⑧

Jennifer could read the words of the spell without thinking. At least without thinking about the words. She *was* thinking – hard. What if one of these times it didn't work? What if she finished and still hadn't reappeared? Or what if the next time she disappeared it was right in the middle of class, or somewhere else in the middle of a crowd of people?

"Faciat invisibilem me experimentum..."

Whatever happened, she made up her mind to miss school that morning. Maggie would have already told them at the office that she was sick. She might as well stay home and get a head start on the watch mystery. And she was convinced that it was connected somehow with her father. Not the fact that the watch was missing, of course, but the watch itself and why it was so important to her mother.

"...Mistletan, Picea, Quercus..." Jennifer stopped.

The phone rang, startling her. It took two rings for her to realize that she could answer it even though she was invisible, and one more to know that she *should* answer it. She was supposed to be here – she was sick. She raced to pick up the receiver before the answering machine caught it.

She recognized Grandma Gagnon's voice on the other end.

"Jennifer! What are you doing home? Sick? Oh my dear what a shame! I hope you feel better soon...I was hoping to catch your mother to find out if she still plans to bring you two out to spend July with us while she takes that Summer School course she needs...has she said anything more to you about it?"

"...N..No...." Jennifer was sure her voice conveyed the right amount of uncertainty. Not a word of a lie, either. Except for the "more" part. Mum had not mentioned the possibility at all. Actually, she and Maggie'd been wondering about summer plans but they'd decided to wait until Mum's exams were over and she wasn't so stressed. Look how upset she'd been just because Jennifer had – well, disappeared. Jennifer glanced at herself in the mirror. The sight of the floating telephone receiver gave her a start. She'd better get back to being visible before her mother came home. "Grandma? Can I have Mum give you a call...I'd better get back to bed. I'm feeling a little...light-headed."

Grandma hung up, all apologies, and Jennifer set down the receiver thoughtfully. Curiouser and curiouser, she thought.

She went back to the spell but her mind wasn't on it. It simply wasn't like her mother to have made plans like that without discussing them with Maggie and her. Mum was really very considerate of them that way. Not like some parents who decided everything and then just told you, as if you didn't have plans and friends and a life of your own.

Grandma's phone call had given her an idea though. She could phone Grandmother Arnold. She might know something about the watch. The last Jennifer had heard from her father's mother had been a postcard from the Yucatán in Mexico. Of course there had been the usual birthday letter with a cheque for each of them to "buy something beautiful for my beautiful grandaughters." Jennifer smiled. It was a perfect excuse to talk to Grandmother Arnold. She hadn't seen Grandmother since the divorce. It was as if her mother had divorced the whole Arnold family. Jennifer didn't think it was fair. She and Maggie were Arnolds too. She would phone Grandmother Arnold the minute she finished.

"...*invisibiliter ut opus hoc qua perficiat mortale...*"

This time the words of the spell caught her just as they had before. Even saying it backwards, the spell had a rhythm that made it easier each time. Jennifer felt confident. Powerful.

"...*Fraxinus, Betula, Salix, Lonicera!*" She finished the words. And sat quietly, eyes closed, waiting.

She did not open her eyes until she felt the now familiar prickling feeling. Fingers and toes first. Then hands and feet. She opened her eyes and breathed a sigh of relief. It had worked again. She wondered briefly how long it would last this time.

"Don't even think about it, Jennifer," she said to herself. "Whatever happens, I'll deal with it *when* it happens. In the meantime..." She smoothed the parchment and put it back in the drawer, changed her mind, took the *Atlas of Alberta* off the shelf and placed the spell inside. Then she slid the slim book under her mattress. Just in case Maggie got any ideas.

She found Grandmother Arnold's phone number in Maggie's address book. To her amazement, instead of the answering service, her Grandmother answered. "You're home!" Jennifer couldn't keep the surprise and delight out of her voice. "It's me...Jennifer."

"Jennifer!" If Grandmother Arnold's voice was any sign, her pleasure at hearing from Jennifer was every bit as great. "Where are you, you sweet girl?"

"Home. I wasn't feeling well this morning...but I'm much better and I'm going to school this afternoon...I just..." Now how do I go about the watch thing? Jennifer wondered.

Grandmother didn't give her a chance. "Alright Darling, you hang up right now and I'll call you back. It's just wonderful to hear your voice, Jennifer, but I've oodles of things to tell you and I don't want your mother to have to pay a big phone bill." Grandmother really did sound overjoyed. "Hang up now."

"Thanks, Grandmother." Jennifer hung up the phone. She should have thought of that. Her mother would kill her when the phone bill came. Making a long distance call without permission would not go over well, whether it was to Grandmother Arnold or anyone else.

The phone rang and Jennifer scooped it up halfway through the first ring.

"That's better. Next time you want to call me, Sweetie, just reverse the charges. Anytime. Anytime, at all."

Jennifer laughed. She'd forgotten how much fun her Grandmother Arnold was. Dad used to refer to her as "your Globetrotting Granny" and Jennifer had always loved the exotic presents and cards she had sent, but most of all it was the sense of fun and excitement that Grandmother seemed to generate. Why had she waited so long to call her?

"Thanks again, Grandmother. I will. How are you? Been anywhere interesting since Chichen Itza? Those Mayan ruins looked really interesting." The postcards had inspired Maggie to get a book on the Yucatán archaeological sites from the library and they'd both poured over it. Jennifer found it very inspiring. If she'd had it a few years earlier when she was nine or ten, she'd have been trying to convince Sam and Maggie to let her use them as human sacrifices.

Grandma laughed, "Oh my yes, I did go sailing in the Caribbean, didn't get a chance to send you a card, the islands we anchored at were very small – Ile aux Saintes, Marie Gabriel, Dominica – places like that. And yes, to answer your question, I'm fine...for an old fogey!"

Jennifer laughed. "Well, I hope I get to be an Old Fogey someday if that's what they do." Last year Grandmother had been whitewater rafting in the Yukon. "So what's next, Grand?" said Jennifer falling back into her own pet name for Grandmother Arnold. When they were little it was decided that Mum's parents would be Grandma and Grandpa, and Dad's mother would be Grandmother – she just didn't fit Granny, although their father had tried to use it as a joke. Jennifer had come up with her own name for her. And really she felt "Grand" was just perfect.

"That's why it's so wonderful that you've called. I'm booking a cruise of the Greek Islands and I was hoping you and Maggie could come with me."

Jennifer hung onto the table. This was glorious news! Absolutely amazing! Wait until Maggie heard about this! "Oh Grand!" she gasped.

"Now don't get too excited yet, Darling Jenny,"

Grandmother's voice was uncommonly cautious, "we have to get your mother's permission. Remember, she wouldn't let you two take the Yucatán trip."

Jennifer was speechless. She was grateful Grandmother couldn't see her face. It was the first she'd heard that they'd even been invited. Why hadn't Mum said anything to them?

"I really don't think it was as dangerous as your mother seemed to think...at the very worst you'd probably only risk a bad case of Montezuma's revenge. But this time, it's perfectly safe – on an American cruise ship, you can live on hamburgers and fries."

Jennifer laughed. "I'm more adventurous than that. Remember the time you took us out for Greek food when we were little and I had the squid!"

"Calamari, Darling Girl...and, yes, no one could ever accuse you of not daring to try something new!"

"I'm sorry we couldn't go to the Yucatán with you. It sounded wonderful!" Jennifer couldn't ignore that one. "After we got your card we got a book about all the Mayan ruins."

"Well, perhaps sometime we can go back. But I think the Greek trip will be even more appropriate. Very educational. We'll spend a few days in Athens, see the Acropolis, the museums and then sail to Crete and look at the Palace of King Minos...you know the story of the Minotaur, don't you?"

Jennifer did. She loved the stories of the Greek myths. This would be a dream come true. Their mother just had to let them go.

The minute the noon buzzer went Maggie decided to find Sam and borrow his cellphone. She had to find out if the spell had worked, or what was more important, lasted. Unfortunately, Sam was nowhere in sight. Ashley Beneton was using hers. Maggie wondered if Ashley was actually talking to anyone. She was tossing her hair and being oh-so-cute and saying over and over, "Oh, I couldn't ...I just *couldn't!*" Maggie decided the performance was solely for the benefit of the two grade nine boys who were watching. She wasn't sure if Ashley would even lend her phone, but she *was* sure that she wouldn't get off the phone until the boys left.

She was standing glaring at Ashley when Sam found her.

"I phoned," he said handing her the cell. "No answer. She's not there. But just to dazzle you with my detecting abilities, I can tell you that the spell worked and Jennifer is on her way."

Maggie looked behind her again. Jennifer had just walked in the door. She'd spotted Ashley and was giving her hair an unsuccessful toss. Then she stopped and walked over to the two grade nine boys and said something. They laughed, shook their heads and talked to her for a minute before she walked away followed by a look of pure poison from Ashley.

Jennifer caught up to them looking mighty pleased.

"So," said Maggie matter-of-factly, "it worked...once more. I'm not even going to ask what you said to those guys. Obviously you did it just to bug Ashley."

"Of course," said Jennifer happily, "and since you're not going to ask, I'll tell you. I simply asked if one of them owned the Porsche in the front lot, because the lights were left on."

"A Porsche in the school parking lot?" Sam looked surprised.

"Don't be silly...but *they* thought it was just fine!" Jennifer did the hair toss again and Maggie noted with satisfaction that she stopped in mid-toss with a tiny grimace of pain. "Anyway," she continued, rubbing her neck as she spoke, "I talked to both Grans...and – Maggie!" Jennifer turned to face her sister stopping so suddenly that Sam nearly ran into her. "Has Mum said anything to you about what we're going to do this summer...where we're going?"

Maggie shook her head. "I supposed we'd go to the lake for a little while, like we always do." Ever since the Gagnon grandparents had sold the farm at St. Paul and retired to a year-round cottage on Lac Ste. Anne, the twins had spent time out there. Maggie had to confess it wasn't quite as much fun now that they were older. Last year she and Jennifer had spent a lot of time trying to think of excuses to stay in the city where there was more happening.

"Did you know that Grandmother Arnold asked Mum to let us go with her on the Yucatán trip?"

Maggie was shocked. Jennifer should have realized that she would tell her if she'd known anything as big as that. "She...what?"

"Yes!" Jennifer said heading for the cafeteria, "And now she wants to take us to Greece...on a cruise...we'll get to see the Palace at Knossos... Remember, the Labyrinth? And the Parthenon and Philip of Macedon's tomb and..."

Maggie could imagine all of it. She kept stopping and hugging herself. This was the feeling Christmas had given her when she was little. She didn't even want to listen or think about the downside. But for once Jennifer was being the practical one and pointing it out.

"What if Mum won't let us go?" Jennifer looked stricken.

"She's got to," Maggie kept repeating, "...she's just got to."

They'd gone through the lineup and reached the cashier now. Maggie realized she hadn't even thought to get a drink, though Sam had and Jennifer was holding a tray with a drink and some chips and gravy. Maggie backed out of line but Jennifer caught her.

"Lend me a dollar, Mag. I'm a bit short of cash." Jennifer was digging in her jeans pocket, pulling out some change. Maggie reluctantly handed her a loonie. Jennifer *never* paid back these loans but sometimes their mother would give Maggie some extra money for lunches. She wouldn't do that for Jennifer – she was trying to train Jennifer to pack lunch for herself.

By the time they'd found a table there was only five minutes before the next class. Maggie watched Jennifer inhale the plate of chips and handed her an apple. Something had occurred to her about the Yucatán trip.

"You know, Jennifer, I guess I can understand why Mum didn't tell us about Grand's wanting to take us...at least if she'd decided we couldn't go."

"Doesn't take a genius to figure that out," Sam put in, "you two would have driven her crazy if you'd known there was the chance of a trip like that!"

"Oh, I know *that*," said Jennifer impatiently. "But why *couldn't* we go? Grand said Mum said it was 'too dangerous.' Why?" Jennifer struck a Wonder Woman pose. "I thrive on danger... Danger...is my middle name...Danger and I..." Jennifer's expression changed suddenly and she clapped her hand over her mouth.

"What's wrong?" Maggie could tell when Jennifer did something for dramatic effect and when she did things for real. This was for real.

Jennifer's face crumbled. "I...I'm starting to feel sick!"

There was no doubt she looked sick *and* very upset.

"You did eat those chips awfully fast," Maggie consoled her.

Sam was quicker to catch on. "Sick? Like you felt the other two times when the spell started to wear off?"

Jennifer nodded unhappily. Maggie slumped in her chair. This was getting worse. One of these times it wouldn't end. Why, oh why? she wondered, couldn't it work the other way? Why couldn't it be that every time Jennifer used the spell to become invisible, it wore off. At least then, Jen would just have to stop using it.

"How long has it been this time?" Sam asked.

Jennifer glanced at her watch unhappily. "A little over two hours."

Sam nodded wisely. "So...the first time was two days, the

second time was overnight, and now we're down to two hours...if we can remember the exact times we should be able to calculate how long the next one will be and..."

Jennifer glared at him. "Never mind," she interrupted. "I'd better get out of here before it happens again. C'mon, Maggie, the washroom.... Now!"

Luckily, there were only two girls in the washroom when they arrived and the buzzer went right away so they were left alone.

"Go ahead, Maggie. Leave me!" Jennifer said with a martyred expression. "We wouldn't want to spoil your perfect record of never being late for class..."

"It's okay. I'll stay," Maggie said sympathetically.

"...Just because," Jennifer continued, obviously feeling sorry for herself, "your sister is in the midst of a major life crisis!"

She never listens to me, Maggie thought, I should just leave her to it. "I said," she repeated, "I'll stay!"

Jennifer looked pleased. "You will? Wow! That's really great of you! Sometimes you are..."

"Never mind the sisterly gratitude," Maggie interrupted. "I've got a spare next period." I should, Maggie thought, have let her think I was being noble. Let her owe me one.

"Say!" said Jennifer, brightening, "why don't we change clothes and you could go to class for me."

"...And the hair?" Not that she would ever agree to this, but Jen should know it wasn't even feasible.

"Simple. Tie a scarf around it and people will just think I've pinned it up." Jennifer threw her backpack on the floor and began to rummage through it. But when she pulled out the scarf to hand it to Maggie, there was a gap between the arm and the scarf because her hand had disappeared.

It took nearly twenty seconds for Jennifer to disappear completely. She had just done so when the door opened and Ashley rushed in, skidded to a stop in front of the mirror and started tucking in her blouse, then pulled out a comb and started on her hair. She ignored Maggie.

Fine, Maggie thought, we'll just get out of here. She went to the door and held it open for Jennifer. It seemed to take Jen longer than it should but finally Maggie felt her going by and started to follow. She was just closing the door when Ashley called.

"This *your* backpack?" she called, looking disparagingly at Jennifer's ratty old backpack.

Maggie didn't say anything, no point in trying to explain that no, it wasn't hers, she wouldn't be caught dead with it. Obviously she was stuck with it. She turned back to pick it up. If she hadn't gone back, she'd never have noticed that the bottom of Ashley's skirt was now tucked into the waistband. Somehow Maggie was sure this wasn't an accident. She turned at the door, "Oh, Ashley," she said sweetly, "your skirt." She left before Ashley could start trying to figure out how that had happened.

SAM 10

S am hadn't made arrangements to meet either of the twins after school. He knew that Jennifer hadn't come back, at least if she had, she never made it to Science class. His last class was French and neither of the girls were in the same class with him.

He decided to take a stroll past Maggie's locker before he left, though, just in case. No Maggie, she must have headed for home already. But the hall was crowded as usual with people leaning against their lockers, eating snacks and the usual slamming and racket.

Ashley Beneton was obviously making progress with Jason Paulus, though. She was leaning against the locker. And Sam had to admit she looked great. Her blonde hair showed up extremely well against the chocolate brown of the lockers. He figured Ashley probably knew that. He was just about to leave when to his amazement a strand of her hair moved snakelike from her shoulder and draped itself across her upper lip. He stared. It really did look as if she had a moustache.

At first Ashley tried to remove it by one of her famous toss-of-the-head moves. When that didn't work she tried blowing it. The moustache stayed. Jason was having a hard time keeping a straight face. Sam couldn't help laughing outright.

Big mistake, he realized, as Jason grabbed him and slammed him against a locker. Sam had given Jason a distraction so he wouldn't get in trouble for laughing at Ashley himself – *and* an opportunity to play hero for her. Jason glared. "What's so funny Dweeb!"

Out of the corner of his eye, Sam noticed Ashley's moustache fall back on her shoulder and the binder she was holding launch itself into the air straight at the back of Jason's head. He waited until impact, then ducked away and headed for the door.

Behind him he could hear Jason's shout of protest as he turned back to Ashley. "What's the big idea, I was sticking up for you!" and Ashley's protest, "But I didn't...Really, I didn't do *anything!*"

Sam flung open one of the double doors. The other one opened at the same time. There was nobody near him so he risked a mumble under his breath, "taking a few chances there weren't you?"

Jennifer's voice was very close. "Don't sweat it, I saved your hide *and* got old Ashley in trouble. A fine day's work."

Sam kept walking, looking straight ahead. He tried to speak without moving his lips too much. At the worst, people would just think he was mumbling to himself. "So, either you didn't go home, the spell didn't work, or it's worn off already." He checked behind him just in case someone was coming who might hear. Nobody. "I hope it was the first."

Jennifer spoke from slightly behind him now. "Right, the first time. It occurred to me that I might as well have a little fun. This thing is turning out to be not all that funny."

Hard to believe how hard it is not to turn your head to face the person you're talking to, Sam thought, but he managed to keep looking straight ahead.

"So," he mumbled, "don't tell me you've been pursuing Ashley for the last two hours."

The voice came from in front of him now. "Nope! I was doing something constructive. Went down to the office and tried to get into my file so I could change all the Lates they've got me down for."

Sam was impressed. "Any luck?"

Jennifer sighed. "No. Either they've got some kind of code to access stuff like that or..."

"...or you should have paid more attention in computer class!" Sam finished for her. "Didn't your mother ever mention," he teased, "that *some* of the things you're supposed to be learning in school *could* prove useful someday!"

"Constantly."

Sam felt a sharp jab in the ribs and resisted the impulse to strike back. Aside from looking ridiculous waving his arms about as he walked alone, he knew his chances of hitting a person he couldn't see were very slim. Knowing Jennifer, he decided, was a great way to develop self-control.

"So," he said, getting serious, "you talked to your Grandmother Arnold. Find out anything about the watch?"

Jennifer had evidently settled down to walking right beside him. "Actually..." she sounded embarrassed, "...I forgot. Well..." she said defensively, "once Grand phoned back...she didn't want me getting in trouble over a big phone bill...and then started talking about the Greek trip, I kind of...forgot about the watch."

"But you did ask about your Dad," Sam said softly.

Jennifer didn't answer right away. Sam supposed she'd nodded. He knew her well enough to know that if the answer had been no, she'd have said it right away. And, if she hadn't wanted to talk about it, she'd have growled something like, "none of your business." Unlike other girls, you knew where you stood with Jennifer – even if, at this particular moment, you didn't quite know where *she* stood.

When she finally answered she was still walking beside him. "Grand said she still didn't know where he was...nothing definite." There was a catch in Jennifer's voice. "That's how she said it, 'nothing definite.' But then, she said something about 'rumours' and having to 'check any leads.'"

Sam felt his arm seized and he was pulled to a halt as Jennifer's voice hissed in his ear. "I think Grand's heard something and the Greek trip is...is to check it out. Maybe the Yucatán one was too."

"Whoa!" Sam breathed, forgetting how he looked standing like that on the sidewalk, staring at nothing at all. "Do you think your Mum knew and that's why she wouldn't let you go? 'Too Dangerous,' she said."

"I don't know, Sam...I just don't know. Maybe it's true...he's being held hostage or something."

Jennifer sounded miserable. Sam knew that she'd worried about that. "You remember? All those kidnappings in Iraq, Hammas or Al Qu...Al...whatever?"

"Al Qaeda. That would hardly explain the Yucatán." Sam noticed that some kids playing in front of a walk-up apartment had stopped and were staring at him, so he started walking again. "Anyway...if it's so dangerous, what's your grandmother Arnold doing chasing around...?"

Jennifer's interruption was indignant. "I'll have you know that Grand was a reporter for *years*. She's been all over the place covering...covering...big...stories!"

Even at the risk of being slugged unexpectedly, Sam could not let that go. "From what your mother said, she spent most of her time working on the *Vancouver Sun* and the only foreign stories she covered were a couple of Royal weddings." He chuckled, "hardly a war zone!" He braced himself, even though he realized that it was hopeless when you couldn't see where your adversary would be striking from. To his surprise, Jennifer began to laugh.

"Oh, I don't know! Haven't you seen pictures of the crowds walking toward Buckingham Palace afterwards?" She giggled harder. "A person could get trampled!" And she was off into gales of laughter.

Nothing to do but wait until she finished, Sam thought. They were just at her house anyway. He waited partly hidden by the hedge. She was probably doubled over by now. He'd seen Jennifer's laughing fits. Sometimes, like this time, it didn't really seem to require anything all that funny.

"OOooo..." she was gasping for breath, "...oooooh ...Oh!...Ouch!"

"Ouch?"

"Ooooh...nothing, really." Jennifer's voice was coming back to normal. She grabbed hold of his arm. "Wait up, I'm having these pins and needles things again in my hands and feet."

Sam had automatically looked down when she'd grabbed him. Now strangely enough he could see fingers and a hand beginning to appear on his arm. It was so spooky it was all he could do not to try to shake the disembodied thing off. It took him a moment to realize that it was Jennifer's hand. She was reappearing before his very eyes. He ducked back further into the hedge pulling her with him, in case anyone drove by.

Good, Maggie thought when she got home, Mum has a seminar on Wednesday nights. "It's okay, I'm alone," she called just in case Jennifer was still invisible.

Maggie was worried. Even if Jennifer had come home, used the spell, and become visible again, it might already have worn off. And, if Sam's theory was correct, she'd be down to seconds of visibility. And then what?

Then it was possible Jennifer was lurking somewhere around the house, waiting to catch her unawares and scare her half to death. Just the sort of thing Jennifer would do.

She walked through every room in the house, listening for Jennifer's breathing, feeling like one of those hapless victims in a horror movie. You know a hand, an axe, or a chainsaw is going to be around the next corner. By the time she'd finished she was in worse shape than if Jennifer *had* jumped out at her.

Funny, Maggie thought, how empty the house seemed. Usually on those rare occasions when she was alone she loved it, revelled in the peacefulness. She decided to curl up on the living-room couch and read. Instead she glanced out of the window and noticed something strange going on. Sam! What on earth was the guy up to? He was hiding in the hedge, some stupid detective thing, no doubt. Probably pretending to have the house under surveillance.

Must be scratchy in there. Wait a minute, he wasn't alone. She could see another set of feet. Jennifer's sneakers. And legs. Maggie raced for the door.

Jennifer was still hiccoughing with laughter as she and Sam came up the steps. Sam was beaming broadly too.

"What's going on?" Maggie demanded. "What was the hedge caper all about? Aren't you two a little old to play those detective games?"

"Look at me!" Jennifer flung her arms in the air in a model pose.

Maggie wasn't impressed. "So," she was disgusted, "you are an exhibitionist, so what?"

"The difference...," said Sam triumphantly, "...is that you can *see* her and she didn't have to use the spell."

Maggie flopped down on the couch. This was good news. "How?"

"I'm not sure," said Jennifer, "but I think it was laughing that did it."

"Now," said Sam seriously, "we just have to figure out what triggers the invisibility. Is there something consistent that happened each time? Think back, Jennifer. What were you doing before you became invisible?"

Jennifer flopped down on the couch beside Maggie. "The first time I had just finished my essay. And the second time I was brushing my teeth and...well...you guys saw the third time, I was eating lunch."

"No similarities in what you were *doing*," Sam mused. "What about how you *felt?*"

"She felt sick...you said that, Jen," put in Maggie. "Queasy, you said, like you were going to throw up or something."

"Symptom," said Sam. "Not necessarily the cause of it," he explained, "just a sign. Like the pins and needles in your hands and feet when you start to reappear each time."

"Well, let's see..." Jennifer concentrated. "The first time, I'd just finished my essay...I was tired...and relieved...."

"How about exuberant?" Maggie suggested. "I always feel pretty good...better than relieved...when I've written a good essay."

Jennifer looked disgusted. "This was *not*, by anybody's standards a *good* essay, most of it came out of other books." She glared at her sister. "And don't look so disapproving, Maggie. It wasn't copying...exactly. I changed most of the sentences...sort of...."

"And this morning?" Sam prompted.

"Cranky!" interrupted Maggie.

"Of course I was cranky. I'm not a morning person!"

Right, Maggie thought, Jennifer in the morning was like a bear whose hibernation had been cut short. She'd been particularly rotten this morning. Maggie had caught her pawing through Maggie's sock drawer like a dog digging up a bone. There'd been a scuffle when Jennifer insisted that the socks she was taking were really hers. It had ended with Maggie yelling, "...and I wouldn't be caught dead with your tatty socks anyway," while Jennifer stormed off to the bathroom.

"And tired," continued Jennifer. "I was tired. Always am in the mornings. Not like little Mary Sunshine over there," she glared at her sister.

"Tired?" said Sam eagerly, then he looked puzzled. "But you weren't tired in the cafeteria. What were you feeling then?"

"Hungry," said Jennifer.

Maggie nodded. Judging by the way those chips had disappeared, Jennifer had been starving. "And excited," she remembered, "you were excited about the trip Grand wanted to take us on."

"Not even a little bit tired, huh?" Sam said sadly. "Or cranky?"

Jennifer shook her head. "Actually," she grinned, "I was feeling pretty good about things. Even aside from the trip stuff and talking to Grand, I did pull a rather good one on Ashley and those boys."

"Not," said Maggie darkly, "that *that* was the worst thing you did to Ashley today." She was not about to elaborate and, judging by Sam's confused look, it seemed likely that the skirt in the washroom was not the only thing that had happened to Ashley while Jennifer was invisible.

Maggie did not want to know.

Sam walked home feeling pleased. He felt that he had come off very well in his interview with Mrs. Arnold. Maybe, he shouldn't call it an "interview" but he still liked the detective game vocabulary that he and Jennifer used when they were kids.

Actually, all he'd been doing was getting the description of the missing watch so that he could run off some notices. He'd got all the basic stuff, gold-filled expansion bracelet, Roman numerals on the face and so on.

He was rather proud of the casual way he'd brought up the question about the engraving. It helped, he was sure, that Jennifer and Maggie had made themselves scarce. Jennifer hadn't been pleased but she'd gone.

"Anything else that might identify the watch?" He said it as if it was an afterthought, as he was about to put his notepad away. And Mrs. Arnold had look startled, then thoughtful, and then wistful, almost sad. He remembered thinking that even if she didn't tell him about the engraving, he was positive that there was one and that it was something personal, even romantic.

Finally she'd smiled and said, "Why yes. Clever Sam. But nobody knew about it, not even the girls. Let's see...there was a date...May 10, 1992, and then the words: 'Love on this happy day' and the initials 'JMA.'" She'd turned away then.

Sam covered the awkward moment by using his best officious TV show cop voice, "And was this inscription in print or script?"

Mrs. Arnold laughed then and said, "You *are* thorough. I don't know about Jennifer, but *you* might just make this detective thing yet! Let's see...the date and initials were in print and the message was script – handwriting."

So, Sam thought, as he fished his key out of an old sneaker piled beside the boots on the porch and unlocked his front door – he'd done very well. He was dying to tell Jennifer. He was sure that she'd be excited. Also she might know the significance of the date. May 10th sounded familiar. And it was – let's see – it was just over thirteen years ago. Thirteen. Of course! He didn't have to ask Jennifer why the date was special. May 10 was the girls' birthday. The watch had been a present when the twins were born. No wonder their mother felt sentimental about it.

And it was something to reassure Jennifer about how much she had meant to her dad. Sam knew that bothered her. After all, he thought, anybody would be bothered to have a father disappear like that and not even try to get in touch with his daughters. Divorce was one thing, but *that* was between the parents. You don't divorce your kids. It may be awkward, but most people stay in touch. Jennifer had waited and hoped for a birthday card this year, though she hadn't said anything. For the week before and even afterwards, she'd been in a hurry to get home from school. Then they'd walk in the door and the first thing she'd do was check the pile of mail on the telephone table in the hall. And then she'd go all quiet, although she never said a word when he asked what was wrong.

There was a note on the kitchen table: "Sam, I'll be home late. There's a TV dinner you can nuke or eat the left-over pizza – if you haven't already."

Sam grinned. His mother knew him pretty well. He'd grabbed the pizza first thing. Before he'd even noticed the note on the table. She should have pinned the note to the pizza if she'd expected him to see it first.

He was just polishing off the last piece, wondering if he'd have room for the TV dinner as well, when the phone rang.

Jennifer's voice on the other end. "Well?" insistent, even angry.

"Yes," he said, then he read the inscription. "That's the day you were born, isn't it?" he asked softly.

Jennifer's voice softened. "Yes. Oh Sam." She was quiet for a moment, then sounded puzzled, "You know, I can't believe she told you about the inscription."

"I asked," said Sam. "I figured if it was a gift...a senti-mental one...that she cared about..."

"Sam!" Jennifer's voice was back to normal even if her words weren't. Jennifer sounded happier than she had in a very long time, Sam thought, as he hung up the phone. How long? Maybe ever since her dad had been gone and Sam just hadn't noticed. Funny. But then that was the way things were. You never really noticed if you were feeling well until you were sick. Maybe he hadn't noticed that Jennifer was unhappy because it had been going on for so long. It took her sounding like this to make him realize.

Somehow, he would have to figure out where her father was. And it would be better if Jennifer didn't even know they were looking. Sam wished he could interview her Grandmother Arnold.

Jennifer had to admit that although Maggie's neatness and habit of carefully planning everything got on her nerves most of the time, when it came to plotting something they both wanted, they were a formidable team.

It had been Maggie's idea to talk to a couple of the teachers *and* the principal about the trip before they began the campaign of persuading their mother to let them go.

Jennifer would have just rushed in relying heavily on the element of surprise, since Mum didn't know they knew there was a chance of such a trip. Then she would have begun a war of attrition – wearing down their mother's resistance by arguing the value of the trip. The arguments would, of course, be interspersed with mournful pleading. "Puhleaze, Mother," accompanied by doggie eyes. Jennifer could do doggie eyes extremely well. She'd learned it very young. And then there was Jennifer's secret weapon. Guilt.

Their mother didn't know they knew she'd turned down the Yucatán trip. And she'd seen them pouring over the books of Mayan ruins. Jennifer was sure that she must have felt guilty about depriving them of such an educational experience.

Guilt was big with single parents. Jennifer had figured this out shortly after the divorce. Comparing notes with classmates, she'd realized that no matter how hard single parents tried to give their children what was needed, they were always afraid that, they'd somehow deprived their children of something they would have had in a two-parent home. Apparently, Jennifer had discovered, the more conscientious the parent, the more they felt this way. And Rita Arnold was very conscientious.

So Jennifer would have just charged in, confronted their mother, and begun her fight to the death. Instead, Maggie planned. First she'd marshalled the teachers. That, as Maggie rightly pointed out, would be the major argument against the trip. True, it was going to be the last week of school and tests should be over, but their mother was a stickler for attendance.

Mr. Wendel, the Social Studies teacher, had been on their side immediately. Of course Maggie was a star pupil but, amazingly, he'd been almost more supportive of Jennifer going. It was, he said, just what she needed to "catch fire" about history. The Language Arts teacher was similarly impressed. As they might have expected, they were to complete reports on what they saw, and do an essay on one particular place, but Jennifer didn't mind that. It would certainly be more interesting than potatoes.

Once they had solved the school problem, Maggie insisted that they do a little background research, so that they could look as if the places they would be seeing were ones they had always longed to visit. A dream come true, not just a nice holiday cruise.

In the meantime, wonder of wonders, four days had passed without accidental invisibility. It was Thursday night before Jennifer had the house to herself. Her mother was at the Library doing research on an essay and Maggie had gone along, ostensibly to do her homework and for company, but really to smuggle back the *Black Book* before it was overdue.

Sometimes Jennifer really was the limit, Maggie thought, as she crawled into bed Sunday night. A person would actually think Jennifer was disappointed that they hadn't had to argue and kick up a fuss to persuade Mum about the trip.

She had given in awfully easily, though. Even Maggie, who'd planned what she considered to be a fool-proof campaign, was a bit surprised.

"Well girls, since it means so much to you, and since my major argument was about school and you've taken care of that very well," Mum had said as the three of them tidied the kitchen after supper, "I can't see any argument to keep you from going –" She'd paused dramatically, but it hadn't had much effect. Her next words had come amidst laughter as the two of them had rushed to hug her. Maggie's "Thanks, Mum" and Jennifer's "Way to go Mum!" had muffled her "You can go!"

By the time Maggie'd come upstairs to bed, Jennifer had piles of packing spread all over the room, including on Maggie's bed which was definitely off limits. It had taken years, but Maggie thought she'd won the battle. Jennifer hadn't trespassed for ages.

It really was too much, Maggie thought, readying herself for a fight. Just when Jennifer should be expressing eternal gratitude for her clever planning.

But the battle fizzled out. Jennifer had scooped everything off Maggie's bed before Maggie even made it across the room. Then the girls had done one of their rare victory dances. Victory dances weren't rare, but usually only one of them was doing the dancing. The other had lost or had nothing to celebrate. This one was mutual and truly triumphant. It ended with them breathlessly falling over – Maggie on her bed, Jennifer dramatically flinging herself into a chair which then tipped over backwards.

It would take quite awhile to settle down and go to sleep, Maggie thought, as she turned out the lights. Lovely to go to sleep when you had wonderful plans to dream of. Maggie usually made up some wonderful dream, even though deep down she knew it would never come true. Now it would. She imagined herself standing on the deck of a sleek white cruise ship, watching the waves of the Aegean breaking against a sun-drenched island.

But just when she felt herself drifting off to sleep, Jennifer intruded.

"Maggie! Are you asleep yet?"

If I was I wouldn't answer, Maggie thought, She decided to hold onto the waves instead.

"C'mon Maggie," Jennifer's voice was insistent. "You can't have gone to sleep that fast. Not tonight."

Trust Jennifer, Maggie thought, I'll bet she's been lying there plotting something all along and getting wider awake instead of trying to settle down and go to sleep. The waves were fading but Maggie wasn't about to give in.

Jennifer tried another tack. "You were brilliant, Mag. Planning everything the way you did. I'd have barged in and blown it with nagging Mum, but your approach was exactly right. Brilliant."

Maggie lost hold of the waves completely. Compliments from Jennifer were rare indeed. She managed to lie still, feigning sleep. Could it be that the only way her sister could manage a bit of appreciation was if she thought Maggie wouldn't hear it?

"You really are talented at planning things..." Jennifer continued.

It's getting a bit thick even for Jennifer, Maggie thought. She's gone beyond a compliment. She wants something. Maggie waited.

"I've been thinking, Mag, do you think we could do it again and take Sam?"

Maggie sat bolt upright. "Are you out of your cotton-pickin' mind?" she all but shouted.

"Sshh," Jennifer hissed. "You'll wake Mum."

"It's nice that somebody gets to sleep around here." Maggie grumbled. "How about showing a little consideration for your brilliant sister."

"I am. If Sam was along, I wouldn't bug you so much. Besides, he makes me laugh which, if this invisibility thing recurs, could be *very* useful.

I knew it was too easy, Maggie thought, Jennifer needs a struggle. She may think she thrives on danger, but really she just thrives on being contrary, swimming upstream, six impossible things before breakfast – stuff like that. Maggie flopped back on the pillow. "You..." she said, giving it a punch, "...are totally insane...utterly mad...completely bonkers...infinitely nuts...truly daft..." Maggie's voice was muffled now as she burrowed her face in the pillow. This could work better than counting sheep, she thought, just thinking of different ways to describe Jennifer. "...Supremely stupid...cosmically cracked..." she mumbled, "...overwhelmingly out-of-it..." She could feel the lovely sleep-feeling coming back.

Click! Jennifer's light was on and Maggie was being shaken.

She couldn't believe it. "...And absolutely assinine!" she almost bellowed. This was too much. "I don't know if Sam will get to go to Greece..." Maggie made a dive for Jennifer. "But you probably won't because I'm going to massacre you."

Jennifer scrambled back into her bed as Maggie hit the floor. "Sssh, you really will wake Mum."

Maggie picked herself up and advanced menacingly toward Jennifer, who was putting on her pleading, doggie look. As if that will work on me, Maggie thought. She's got to be kidding, it just looks ridiculous. "Rampantly ridiculous...and..." Maggie snarled as she stood glaring down at her sister. She was having trouble keeping a straight face. Jennifer looked so "...supremely silly!"

"How about delightfully doggie?" said Jennifer and then they were both laughing, howling and rolling about on Jennifer's bed where Maggie had fallen.

Which was where their mother found them when she opened the door a few moments later. "I know you two are too excited to go to sleep right away," she said sympathetically, "but could you just talk quietly. I've got an exam in the morning!"

Maggie was instantly contrite, Jennifer did her doggie bit. "Sorry Mum," they said in unison as their mother closed the door behind her.

"Now that you're wide awake," said Jennifer as Maggie climbed back into bed, "and we have permission to talk quietly for a while, could you put your mighty mind onto getting Sam on the trip?"

Maggie sighed. There was just no resisting Jennifer. She was like one of those big things that used to run over people – what was it? A juggernaut. She could see her sister staring eagerly back at her. Jubilantly juggernautish, she thought. Six impossible things before breakfast, and Maggie at midnight. "Look Jen, I'd be the first to admit that it would be very nice if Sam could come along. But you're overlooking a couple of *very* important details." She counted on her fingers. "First and *most* important, there's Grand to think of. She's being quite splendidly generous taking *us* along –"

"I know," Jennifer interrupted, "and I'll phone her first thing in the morning and she won't have to...."

"Then," continued Maggie using her next finger, "there's the matter of money...plane fare getting there *and* the cruise."

"Yes, but..." Jennifer began.

Maggie cut her off. She was speaking faster now, counting off fingers before Jen could butt in again.

"And what about his parents? What about school? Doesn't he usually spend part of the summer with his grandfather in the Maritimes?" Maggie was running out of reasons but it didn't matter. Even if everything else could be worked out, the money was the big one. That was impossible.

Jennifer had stopped trying to interrupt and was waiting for Maggie to finish.

Sam was standing on the edge of the bathtub with his head pressed against the tiles. From that angle he could see Jennifer and Maggie's window. Not enough to see into the room, but enough to see that the light was still on. It was late for them to be up, Mrs. Arnold was strict about lights out and she had an eight o'clock class Monday morning.

The light on meant just one thing. Jennifer was telling Maggie about taking him. He grinned as he stepped down into the tub. He could just imagine Maggie's reaction. Right now she was probably listing every practical excuse why it was impossible.

Well, he and Jennifer had been over every one he could think of. The big one – getting there – had been relatively easy, even though he'd just learned about it the other day. There'd been a letter from the Elwin grandparents in Devonshire, England last week, inviting him to spend a week or two with them this summer – they'd even offered to send the plane fare.

"Not that they can't afford it," his dad had said when he read the letter. "What do you think of that, Sam, old boy?"

His father got all English whenever letters came from "the Brit Grandparents." Sometimes, Sam thought, it was really funny, especially since Dad had really been born in Canada and had grown up here, and talked as Canadian as anybody, most of the time. The Elwins had only gone back to England when Grandfather had retired ten years ago.

Sam wasn't sure what he thought about the trip. He'd only visited them once, five years ago, and that was with his parents. He didn't really remember his grandparents from when they lived in Canada, and the visit had been extremely boring for an eight-year-old. Tea cosies, cucumber sandwiches, and lots of dull talk about relatives he'd never met and didn't particularly want to meet once he heard about them.

The only thing that made the trip exciting was that London was over halfway to Greece and Jennifer and Maggie would be changing planes there on their way to Athens. If he had a ticket to London, he was on his way.

"I'd love to go," he said.

When they'd told his mother, she'd suggested that he might as well visit her father at the same time. Sam visited him every summer. That was always fun. Grandad Martell was much younger than his Elwin grandparents. He taught Classics at the University in Wolfville, except this year he was on sabbatical doing research on the Etruscans, in Italy. Sam hadn't dared hope he'd get to visit him this year – in fact he'd been dreading the long boring summer – especially since he found out Maggie and Jennifer wouldn't be around. But now with a free trip to England, his mother said she thought they could arrange a visit to Grandad as well.

"I'll phone right now...let's see, what time is it there?"

Of course, Grandad was delighted. And Sam began to hope. Two weeks in Greece first, then Rome, Volterra actually, and then a peaceful week in Devon. With a stack of books, it wouldn't be so bad.

It had been at this point that he and Jennifer had started to plan.

"No problem convincing Grand to take you. She's liked you ever since you were little," Jennifer pointed out. "She used to call you Sam Gamgee and we never knew why until we got old enough to read *Lord of the Rings.*"

No, the major problem would be paying for the cruise. But even that wasn't as big a problem as it might have been. There was money, a few thousand dollars that Sam had inherited from his great-grandfather Martell. Grandad Martell was the trustee and Sam was sure that he'd approve of anything that had to do with learning about ancient Greece. He'd e-mailed immediately.

Sam turned off his computer before he slid into bed. It was late but his parents didn't care what time he went to bed, as long as he got up and got to school on time.

He had some thinking to do. He needed to study the list he'd printed out. Invisibility. He'd listed the events surrounding each occurrence. Now that they knew about the laughing he was sure that there was a common denominator in what caused the invisibility too – but what? Staring at the list didn't help. Maybe it would make sense in the morning, he decided as he turned out the light.

It seemed like a miracle the way things were falling into place. First the trip to England, and then visiting Grandad in Italy. He was sure Jen could persuade her Grandmother Arnold to take him. And even the money for the cruise was possible. He hadn't told Jennifer, but there was another problem. Cabins. Jennifer and Maggie could share one or share with their grandmother. But Sam was on his own and he'd looked at the cruise magazines Maggie picked up at a travel agency. The fare to occupy a cabin by yourself was almost twice as expensive as to share one. Which meant Sam would have to share a cabin with a stranger, and he wasn't sure his mother would go along with that. No, actually he was sure – she wouldn't, and that would be that.

Jennifer woke up feeling wonderful. The whole, cranky morning thing seemed just a memory. "O what a beautiful morning," she sang as she waltzed to the bathroom.

Actually, she thought, as she saw the look on Maggie's face coming out of the bathroom, it's worth faking it just to get that reaction from Muggins. "Good morning, Maggie, you dear, sweet, *brilliant* sister you."

Maggie's puzzled look changed to a grimace. "Listen, Jennifer, just because you shot down all my arguments about Sam coming along, doesn't mean it's going to work." She started counting on her fingers, "there's still the school thing *and* his parents *and* Grand *and....*"

Jennifer cut her off by slamming the bathroom door in her face and turning on the sink taps full blast. "Details..." she yelled merrily, "...mere details...."

She skipped downstairs and found her mother rushing back in from the car. "Jennifer! Did you see my Ed. Psych textbook when you tidied the living room yesterday?"

"Nnno..." she mumbled, "...why?" Jennifer had a sinking feeling. She hadn't exactly "tidied" the living room. She'd grabbed everything, books, newspapers – everything – and just dumped it behind the couch. She meant to put the stuff away later but she'd forgotten.

"I thought I'd put it in my briefcase...but it's not there...and this is an open-book exam and..." Her mother was already halfway up the stairs.

Jennifer was already hanging over the back of the couch. Yes, there was one of Mum's textbooks in the heap of stuff behind the couch. She grabbed the book, rushed to the front hallway and tossed it on the chair by the coat closet. She just made it back into the living room as her mother came down the stairs. Jennifer hoped that she looked as if she was just standing looking at the chair in the hall. "Is that it?" she asked, pointing.

Her mother looked puzzled. "That's strange," she said, "I should have noticed it there."

"Umm..." Jennifer said. Luckily it was easy for her to look guilty. "I had my sweater on the chair...and you must have..." her voice trailed off.

She was off the hook. Her mother had already grabbed the book and was heading out. "Thanks, Jennifer. I'm just so glad I checked my briefcase before I left...." Her voice was fading as she rushed to the back door, "...I'd have been in terrible trouble without it...I can't believe I didn't see it on the chair...." was the last thing Jennifer heard as the door slammed.

Jennifer's feeling of elation had gone. Even relief at her narrow escape, didn't help. Mum worked really hard and if she'd missed her book at the exam and flunked it would have been Jen's fault.

Maggie was standing at the kitchen door and had seen the whole thing. "Well you weaseled out of that one," she said disapprovingly. "You told Mum a bold-faced lie, Jennifer."

Jennifer didn't bother to answer. She felt bad enough. She didn't need an argument with Maggie as well. She brushed past Maggie and went into the kitchen. For once there was time for breakfast, but she really didn't think she could eat.

She was standing staring into the fridge when Maggie came in and started putting some bread in the toaster. Just the sight of food made her feel sick, the smell of the toast was too much. She closed the fridge and flopped down at the kitchen table. Maybe if she sat very still it would go away. She was just starting to feel better, when there was a crash. Maggie had turned away from the counter, started toward the table and suddenly dropped the plate of toast she'd buttered.

"Jennifer! You're disappearing again!"

At least that explained the feeling sick part, Jennifer thought, looking down to where her arms and hands should be. Fade out time again, she thought miserably. That's all I need.

She heard Sam's special knock on the kitchen door and Maggie yelled, "Come in!"

Sam stared at what was left of Jennifer, then he stooped to pick up one of the fallen slices of toast, blew on it and sat down opposite her.

"That's been on the floor," said Maggie, picking up the broken plate and throwing it and the other slice of toast in the garbage.

"I noticed," said Sam taking a bite. "My mother always says that you could eat off your mother's floors." He stared at where Jennifer had been. "So! Were you cranky again this morning?"

Jennifer shook her head and then realized that didn't help.

"No," Maggie said handing Sam a bowl of Shreddies, "as a matter of fact, she was a regular Little Mary Sunshine this morning."

"Hmmm...." Sam looked interested. "...Not cranky. What about tired?"

Jennifer started to shake her head no, and then said it instead.

"So," said Sam, "it's just like the time with Ashley. Exactly what did you do?"

"She lied to Mum," Maggie had her mouth full of cereal but she answered before Jennifer had a chance.

"I fibbed, Maggie. A fib is when you don't want to upset somebody...it wouldn't have done any good to say I hadn't cleaned the room properly and her Psych book accidentally got dropped out of sight...now would it?" Jennifer was beginning to resent Maggie's righteous attitude. "Anyway, I found it for her, so no harm done." Jennifer cut her sister off, "and you don't have to remind me that it could have been really bad if Mum hadn't missed the book before she left for the exam."

"Let me get this straight," Sam said pulling out his notebook, "you've gone invisible accidentally four times in all."

"Right," Maggie put in counting on her fingers. "Once after the essay..."

"The second time after being cranky in the morning..." added Sam.

"...And messing around with my socks...."

"...and a fight with Maggie," Sam noted. "The third time with Ashley and the Porsche story...."

"Right!" said Jennifer unhappily, "And now."

"Number four: lies...er...fibs to mother." Sam continued.

Jennifer went to the fridge to get some orange juice. It was gratifying to see Maggie and Sam jump when she slammed the door. They both watched, fascinated as she carried the glass back to the table. Wonderful, Jennifer thought, even from her point of view it seemed to be floating across the room by itself. "So, Sherlock," she said sarcastically as she sat down. "What do the 'little grey cells' tell you?"

"That's not Sherlock, that's Poirot..." Sam began.

Jennifer slammed her fist on the table. Again the other two jumped. Their expressions were so silly. She was tempted to startle them again. "Never mind that... *what* do you *conclude?*"

She had to admit Sam was cool. He was staring straight at her even though he couldn't see her.

"Number one," he said, "Essay – you might say you cheated, copying stuff and hardly changing it. Number two, did you *really* think your socks were in Maggie's drawer?" Sam was doing his best Perry Mason imitation. "Number three, was there really a Porsche with its lights on in the parking lot? In other words, Jennifer, each time there was one thing in common...."

Sam paused for effect and Jennifer knew he was on the right track so she beat him to it. "I lied...well...fibbed, each time," she said in a flat voice. She hated to admit it but Sam must be right. Still it was a relief.

"Right," said Sam, glaring at her. "Which means that now you can prevent it."

"Which means," Maggie said, smiling widely, "That Jennifer's got to tell the truth or we'll know when she's lying!"

Jennifer groaned. Maggie was right. Still, she did feel relieved. Now that she knew how to handle it she'd be able to become invisible and visible again without even using the spell. Let Maggie laugh all she wanted. Jennifer would have the last laugh. And speaking of that, there was just one more thing. She glanced at the clock. It was almost time for them to leave for school.

"So...Sam..." she said turning toward him. "Heard any good jokes lately?"

Jennifer was waiting by his locker after school. She was amusing herself by tearing a sheet of paper into confetti-sized pieces and sliding them through the slots of Ashley's locker. Very neatly too, Sam had to admit. Nobody would have realized it to look at her. She was casually leaning against the locker between Sam's and Ashley's and her backpack was screening what her hands were doing behind her back from anybody nearby. Sam only realized what she was up to when he opened his locker and glanced over. Mind you, he thought, the casual innocence of Jennifer's expression should have given it away. If Jennifer was looking innocent – look out!

"So...have there been any responses to the watch flyers?" he asked as they left the school. Actually he was sure he knew the answer to that one anyway. Jennifer would have told him if there'd been anything.

"Nope." Jennifer shook her head. "I know a good detective never gives up, but this was pretty impossible. Mum's right, the clasp probably broke and it fell off and she didn't notice it."

"I expect you're right...it was one of those old-fashioned wraparound type clasps...wasn't it?"

"Yeah...a funny little double-hook kind of end that snapped around the bracelet...." Jennifer stopped suddenly. "Sam! I've seen that somewhere...just the clasp and it didn't register at the time...you know when you see something that doesn't quite make sense because you're doing something else and you don't..."

"Okay." Sam was being calm, but there was no doubt about it, Jennifer was obviously onto something. "Shut your eyes and try to picture the clasp as you saw it."

"I didn't even realize it *was* the clasp until now, thought it was a broken earring or something...it was lying some-where.... I was sort of peeking...didn't get a good view..." Jennifer's eyes popped wide open. "Behind the couch!" she said triumphantly. "Lying on the floor with the newspapers and stuff I dumped back there." She started walking again. "No wonder I didn't stop to pay any attention, all I needed to do was get that book out of there, fast!"

"Well, if the clasp was there, chances are pretty good that the watch is too. Maybe not on the couch, your mother probably looked there, but if the clasp fell behind, the watch might have dropped there too." They turned in at their respective houses. "Phone me after you've checked." Sam called.

He wanted to check his e-mail to see if Grandad had answered him. He fished out the door key and had just managed to get inside when the phone began to ring.

That was fast, he thought as he answered, but it wasn't Jennifer at all. It was long distance from Italy.

"You never told me you were so interested in Ancient Greece, Sam, but then even if you weren't this sounds like a wonderful introduction! Have you talked to your parents about this yet?"

Sam could be honest with Grandad, "No, I figured they'd just say it was too expensive and where would I get the money and..." He took a deep breath, "...and if you agreed then they would too!"

Grandad laughed. "Smart boy! I expect you're right. Well, I agree, but..."

Sam's heart sank. If Grandad had a "but," it could be a problem.

"It's much too expensive if you have to have a cabin by yourself. Most people book a cabin for two or have to accept whoever the cruise line makes them share with. Sometimes that works fine but sometimes it can be...awkward."

Sam nodded, "I wouldn't mind, I'd be out on deck or ashore most of the time and..." He was trying to make his voice sound as eager as he could. Minimize the problem – that was the only way, otherwise the whole thing was hopeless. And just when he was getting so close. "...there's got to be a way, Grandad." He knew his voice was starting to sound desperate.

"Well," Grandad's voice was calming, "I'm sure there's something. Too bad I'm committed to the work I'm doing here. I wouldn't mind going. Unfortunately, it's out of the question. Do you know which cruise line it is?"

Sam was annoyed. He knew Maggie had told him but there'd been all those other catalogues and now he couldn't remember which one the girls were going on. "Nnno..." he said, "but they've got special guides and lectures about the places." It would have been wonderful if Grandad could have gone, but at least Sam knew enough not to get his hopes up about that.

"That's why I was asking," said his grandfather, "one of my colleagues here is going to be doing those lectures for the Princess cruise which goes about the same time. He's travelling alone and if it's the same ship, you could probably share a cabin with him."

Not as wonderful as sharing with Grandad, but a solution. "I don't think that's it, but I'll check."

"Find out, Sam, and I'll do some checking, I'll phone you back on Sunday. If you like I'll break the news to your parents then. And Sam," Grandad added, "don't worry. We'll work it out. It's a great opportunity. Very, very nice of the girls' grandmother to offer to take you along."

Sam hung up. Things were going very well, but there was more than one problem. Jennifer hadn't even asked her grandmother yet as far as he knew.

Maggie was sitting at the kitchen table doing homework when she heard Jennifer slam the front door. She braced herself for the entry of Hurricane Jennifer but it didn't happen. Instead there were thumping and rustling sounds in the living room. Maggie heaved a sigh and stood up. She'd better go and see what Jen was up to now – sometimes she really felt like Jiminy Cricket to Jennifer's Pinocchio.

"After this morning," she began, "you'd think that you would have learned..." She stopped. Jennifer was bum up hanging over the back of the couch tossing newspapers and magazines out into the room. "What *are* you doing?"

"I, " Jennifer said, "am solving the mystery of the missing watch – *that's* what I'm doing." She waved something she was holding in her hand. "Exhibit A – the broken clasp."

Maggie crossed the room and peered behind the couch

"Nothing!" Jennifer looked dejected. "But it's got to be near by." She held out her hand again, this time Maggie could see the broken clasp on her palm.

"It might help..." Maggie was already tugging at the couch, "if we pulled this away from the wall."

Together they succeeded in moving the heavy furniture. Jennifer had pulled off the cushions and was reaching down the sides of the couch while Maggie crawled in behind. The floor was clear of all but a box of Kleenex. "We may have to pull this out a bit more." She stuck her head around the end of the couch. Jennifer was standing in the middle of the room shaking newspapers and throwing them aside. "Never mind, maybe I...." Maggie slid her fingers along the bottom edge of the couch. There was something there. "Eureka!" she said.

"You what?"

"Eureka!" Maggie repeated. "That's Greek for 'I found it,' at least I think it is...there's a story of some ancient Greek and a bathtub and...oh, never mind, look it up some time. Look!" she said. She waved the watch in Jennifer's face as she peered over the back of the couch at her.

"That's it!" Jennifer reached out and turned the watch over to read the inscription.

"Love on this Happy Day, JMA," she read out loud. "May 10, 1992."

Maggie made a grab for the watch. She hadn't known there was an inscription. "May 10, 1992." She caught her breath and her eyes filled with tears. "He gave it to her when we were born," she breathed.

She could see Jennifer nodding through the blur and hear her saying something and then Jennifer was crying too. Maggie held up the Kleenex box and they were wiping their eyes and blowing their noses. Jennifer had the hiccoughs.

"You knew?" Maggie asked. "About the inscription?" Jennifer nodded. "Why didn't you tell me?"

"I didn't know you...*hic*...would care...you didn't...*hic* even seem to notice when Dad dis...dis...*hic*...was gone."

Maggie felt as if somebody had hit her in the chest. Is that what Jennifer had been thinking all this time? That she didn't care? She just sat staring up at her sister, her eyes filled with tears again.

Jennifer reached down and squeezed her shoulder. "Sorry Mag...I just...I tried to talk to you about it and..."

Funny, Maggie thought, that whenever they didn't understand each other it was over something major. "It's just," she said, "that I sort of believe Grandma Gagnon's saying, 'Don't worry about problems. There are only two kinds: those you can solve and those you can't. You don't need to worry about the ones you can solve, just solve them. And if you can't do anything about the other problems there's no point in worrying about them.' I figured I couldn't do anything about Dad and Mum and why he didn't come around anymore." She stopped. She could see Jennifer's point. To somebody else, it might look as if she just didn't care. She grabbed another Kleenex.

"Well," said Jennifer, "I do worry. But maybe it still fits. We are going to do something. You see, I think..."

Maggie would have to wait to find out. The front door opened and Jennifer jumped up as the angry voice of their mother cut in. "What do you think you're doing!"

Maggie, cringed. Newspapers and cushions everywhere, furniture askew – it didn't look good alright.

"Jennifer Arnold, what do you think you're doing! I doubt that you've got any kind of an explanation, *or* that I'll believe it for a minute when I hear it, but...."

From where she sat behind the couch she could see

Jennifer standing looking guilty. Once in awhile, not often, when she did something really serious, she'd actually be at a loss for words. Maggie knew she'd better step in. "You see Mum, it's like this..." she stood up "We were having one more look..."

"Maggie?" Mum looked shocked as Maggie popped into view. "What are *you* doing here?"

The tone of voice was much gentler. Even as she began to answer Maggie realized with a shock that Jennifer was right about the way their mother responded differently to each of them. Maggie was being given the benefit of the doubt here – Jennifer was guilty until proven innocent.

"We decided to do one last search for the watch. Jennifer thought she'd glimpsed the clasp this morning...."

Jennifer'd recovered enough to add, "...and Maggie thought maybe when it broke the watch might have fallen...."

"...And it had," Maggie said as she held up the watch. "We'll clean up." No point in talking anymore. The look on Mum's face was enough as she held out her hand for her watch.

"I...I'm sorry I yelled at you Jennifer," she said softly. She didn't say any more, just gave them both a long hug. "Thank you very much." Her voice returned to its usual matter-of-fact tone, "so...I guess this means we split the reward between the two of you."

Maggie nodded.

"And Sam," said Jennifer. "And speaking of Sam," she said, staring at Maggie, "I've got to make a phone call."

"First," said their mother, "you'll clean up the mess."

Jennifer didn't have a chance to put in the call to Grand about Sam until she got home from school the next day. Actually, she thought, it didn't hurt that she'd waited. Now she could mention that Sam's grandfather was working on arranging the cruise part of it.

"Of course Grand, it's up to you. I know it's a big thing to ask...another person for you to look after...."

"Oh I'm sure Sam Gamgee will be no problem. My objections would be exactly the things it seems his grandfather is sorting out. What do his parents say to it?"

Jennifer hesitated, "...ummm...actually Grand, they don't know yet...we had to ask you first...and get his grandfather on our side...I mean..."

Jennifer could hear Grand laughing. "You are clever plotters. I suppose you're going to let the grandad break the news to the Elwins?"

No point in trying to fool Grand. Jennifer laughed, "Got it in one! He's supposed to tell them when he phones back on Sunday."

"Well," said Grand, "since it's a grandparent plot, you'd better get his phone number. I'll phone Italy and give him the details of the cruise, then we can either book it through my travel agent or he can arrange it from there."

Lovely, just lovely, thought Jennifer. "I take it this means a yes?" she laughed.

Grand laughed too. "I'm really looking forward to spending some time alone with you, and with Sam there Maggie won't feel abandoned. I've got some things to tell you, things I...things I can't really say on the phone. It's been a long time since we've been together."

It has, Jennifer thought, as she hung up. The last time they'd visited Grand had been with Dad, just before he left for the job in the Middle East.

So, she wondered as she headed for class, she wants to talk to me alone. What about? About Dad, she hoped, something about him that she would tell only Jennifer? Whatever it was, the mere fact that Grand wanted to talk to her about it made her feel very special. She couldn't wait for June, the end of school, and this trip to begin.

She walked home alone that day. Maggie was staying to help in the library and Sam had to go to the dentist. No problem. It gave her a chance to think.

She still hadn't had a chance to get together with Sam and test the invisibility thing. It would be great when she had it under control and could actually use it. She hadn't dared to so far, it seemed to call for something important, not just playing tricks on Ashley. And she wanted to be able to use it. Somehow she thought it might come in very handy on the trip. There'd been something in Grand's voice this morning. Had she found out where Dad was? Something so secret it couldn't be spoken about over the phone? Maybe it was just that it would take too long – that they needed to sit down and that her grandmother had a lot to say. Was that all?

She spotted Sam getting off the bus at the end of the block and broke into a run.

"So," she said out of the side of her mouth, as she came up beside him, "did you talk?"

"Naw...they tortured me," he mumbled back, "but I didn't give them the secret formula, I didn't tell them a thing. Except, of course," he broke character and grinned at her, "your name!"

"Thanks, a lot!" She laughed as he turned into his driveway. "By the way, Mrs. MacNeil wants to talk to you first thing in the morning. I think you're in trouble." That was mean, thought Jennifer as she saw the worried look on Sam's face, but if I don't disappear on that one, nothing will do it. She'd phone Sam in a few minutes and tell him the truth, regardless of the result.

Her mother was coming down the stairs. Jennifer's heart sank. There wasn't supposed to be anyone home. Then she remembered. It was exam week at University. Mum stuck to her class and study schedule like a fanatic and Jennifer'd grown so used to knowing when she would be gone, that she'd forgotten things would be different this week. There was probably a schedule posted on the fridge and Jennifer hadn't been paying attention when Mum told them about it. Oh, Oh! She was starting to feel queasy. The lie had worked.

"Jennifer what's the matter, you don't look well."

In two minutes her mother would have her in bed. "No...I'm fine," she said, turning back towards the door. "I forgot to tell Sam something...a message from one of the teachers.... He's got to talk to..." Her hand was on the door-knob. She looked down. Good, it was still there. "I won't be long," she said. She closed the door quickly before her mother could respond.

She ducked around the back to Sam's kitchen door. She didn't want to disappear on his front step waiting for him to come to the door.

Sam opened the door looking puzzled. He'd obviously just taken a bite out of the piece of pizza in his hand. If "you are what you eat" had any truth to it, Jennifer thought as she slipped by him, Sam would be a giant pizza any day now.

"Are you alone?"

Sam looked a little put out. "Of course," he said. "I'm the only one who lives here – you know that!"

Jennifer felt a moment's sympathy. He was always alone. His parents worked downtown and often met for a drink after work. Usually they'd end up having dinner afterwards while Sam foraged for himself.

"I need to sit down," she said, flopping on a kitchen chair.

"You don't have any chairs at home?" He'd turned and was getting the milk out of the fridge.

"Yep," Jennifer said. "But my mother's there and I didn't want to have to say 'Look Maw, no hands!'"

When he turned around she was holding up her arms which now seemed to end at the elbows.

"Okay!" he said matter-of-factly, "what was the lie?" The light dawned in his face. "Mrs MacNeil doesn't want to see me...Jennifer that was rotten!"

Jennifer hung what was left of her head. "I'm sorry, I was going to phone you when I got in the house. Mum surprised me by being home." She smiled at him and then realized that he couldn't see her do it. "Okay, I won't do it again...it's just I really wanted to give the lie thing a real test." She tried to put as much appeal into her voice as she could, knowing that no matter how contrite she looked he wouldn't get the effect of it. "But I've got good news! Everything's okay with Grand about you coming. She even wants your grandfather's phone number so that she can talk directly to him about the arrangements."

Sam grabbed the phone directory by the counter phone and started writing down a number.

"You know," he said. "We could save a lot of money and trouble, if I'd just used the spell and taken the trip while invisible. I mean, now that we know how to use it."

Jennifer shook her head, then stopped, she'd never realized before how much she relied on gestures. "No good," she said. "For one thing, we only know how it might work with me. For another, we still don't know what would happen with long-term invisibility...are there other factors other than laughing that can reverse the spell? Does it just wear off? Imagine suddenly appearing in the midst of an airline terminal or going through customs. Besides, how would you eat? You might be able to sneak some food if you were alone, but on an eight-hour plane trip in a plane full of people...and what about on board ship? You'd have to sleep and you'd need a key to get into a cabin...."

"Okay, okay!" Sam stopped her. He was looking at her, shaking his head. "You know," he said laughing, "sometimes you and Maggie aren't so different after all. You wouldn't happen to be counting on your fingers would you?"

"Fingers? What fingers?" said Jennifer and began to laugh.

t seemed to Maggie that Jennifer must have packed and repacked a dozen times since that first night. No, on second thought, it would be impossible to count. It had been more like a continuous packing and unpacking. Sort of like that Greek queen, who did her weaving each day and then unravelled it each night because she'd promised that she'd choose one of her suitors to marry when she finished, but if she never finished she didn't have to marry.

Even Maggie was packing now. Neatly folded piles of clothes covered her bed and dresser. She'd begun, of course, making a list of exactly what she needed to take: toothbrush, toothpaste, exactly how many pairs of panties she should need (seven), and how many pairs of shoes (runners, sandals, canvas slip-ons, thongs, and the beige leather ones that would go with her sundress or her new party one). She consulted the list again. Shampoo and conditioner. She'd just take a combination. It looked like Jennifer had an entire drugstore piled on her bed: spray and mousse and bubble bath and shower gel. Nice going Jen, Maggie thought. At least she'd persuaded her to jettison the hair dryer. No telling what kind of plug-ins there'd be. Anyway, Grand had said they could use her hair dryer with the universal plug attachment.

Unfortunately, all the space Maggie was saving on being so organized was being taken up by books. The pile of books she had decided to take – she could picture herself lying on a deck chair caressed by the soft Aegean breezes reading and looking like some exotic foreign film star – seemed to be growing daily. Every Madeleine L'Engle and Monica Hughes she could find was there. And of course, there were several books on Greek history and some Mary Renault that Grand had sent.

Less than a week and they'd be on the plane to Vancouver. One more week and that wonderful Greek sunshine she'd been dreaming about would be beaming down on her head.

"Hats!" she cried as Jennifer came in. "We've forgotten hats!"

"Speak for yourself," Jennifer said, digging into one of the crammed suitcases on the floor beside her bed. She flourished a red tam, a navy Tilley hat, a floppy black velvet hat with a huge sunflower, and a cotton-knit disaster in shocking pink. "I've got a couple more..." she looked ruefully at the tangle of clothes in the suitcases, "...somewhere."

Maggie just shook her head. It was useless to say anything. The last time she made a comment, Jennifer had pointed out that she was saving space because she was only taking two sets of underwear since she could wash them out every night. Big deal.

"Oh, by the way," Jennifer said as the doorbell rang, "Sam's coming over. He got an e-mail from his grandad...more about the mystery roommate!"

They'd been wondering about the problem of Sam sharing a cabin with some unknown man. Well, not exactly unknown. Dr. Martell had arranged for him to be put in the cabin of the classical archaeologist who'd been hired to give lectures about the various ancient sites. Unfortunately, they weren't going on the ship his friend was on, and Sam's grandfather didn't know the man.

Sam flopped down on the couch in the TV room and pulled out the e-mail he'd printed off.

"Grandad says," he said, beginning to read, "I still have not been able to get much information on Dr. Rossi, except that he studied at the Oriental Institute in Chicago and taught at a couple of midwestern colleges in the US – and Kansas State University was one of them. Luckily, one of the archaeologists here was there at the same time and knows him slightly. Unfortunately, he is mainly aware of Rossi's academic credentials, which seem to be fairly good. Personally he didn't know the man that well, nor does he know very much about his personal life, except that he travelled a good deal and was either single or divorced."

"Does he have any children?" Jennifer interrupted.

"Grandad doesn't say and I guess he would have if this man he knows knew of them." Sam read on. "He's been doing the cruise thing periodically over the years, according to my colleague, and so we have to assume that he's alright. Not much of a talker, my friend said, but pleasant enough. You shouldn't have any problems." Sam looked up from the letter. "I won't be hanging around the cabin anyway, I'll be with you two...and your grandmother...."

"Right," said Jennifer. "So that settles it. Your mother isn't going to fuss?"

"Bit late now," Sam laughed, "Grandad had to get the ticket right away, apparently the only chance of getting on the ship was to persuade Dr. Rossi to share a cabin. Staff don't usually share with passengers, but Dr. Rossi agreed after Grandad talked to him. Anyway he's not exactly staff, just does the lectures. Grandad said all the shore tours have to be booked through the local tourist agencies."

Jennifer raised an imaginary magnifying glass to her eye and assumed her Sherlock Holmes pose, "Well, I for one am going to keep my eye on him, Watson!"

"That ought to make him wish he'd stayed at home," Maggie said drily. She hoped Jennifer wouldn't embarrass her with silly detective games on board the ship. The fact that they were identical could be a real problem. She often caught people looking at her strangely or even asking her why she'd done something stupid that she hadn't done. Nobody believed there were two of them unless they saw them together and saw their different hair styles. She'd make a point of sticking with Jennifer constantly the first few days on board ship, just to make sure people caught on to the idea of twins.

PART 2

THE ADVENTURE BEGINS

JENNIFER 21

Jennifer stood in the arrivals area of the Athens Airport and watched the people filing by her on the way to claim their luggage. Maggie and Grand had left her to go to the bathroom. Somebody had to stay. Sam was supposed to be getting off the flight from Rome any minute now. He'd be with his grandfather's friend, but so far she couldn't see any sign of him.

They'd been in Athens for a week and tomorrow they sailed. For a wonderful week they'd wandered through the ruins around the Temple of Hephaestus, and the old Roman Agora.

They'd climbed up to the Acropolis, seen the Parthenon and the ruins there. Jennifer had stood there in the sunshine, the city of Athens stretching in all directions, and tried to imagine what it must have been like before most of it fell down or was destroyed or carried off to museums around the world. There was only a tiny piece of the Parthenon frieze left on – bits of a man and a horse – but there was a reproduction in the museum so she had an idea of how wonderful it must have been. All three of them had taken turns snapping pictures in front, but it was so windy Jennifer couldn't keep the hair out of her face.

She and Maggie had better luck taking each other's pictures with the Caryatids. Lovely statues of women holding the roof of a temple up with their heads. Jennifer had posed holding her head as if she was commiserating about headache. She'd worked hard getting Maggie to stand just far enough away so that she'd seem to be exactly the same size as one of the Caryatids.

They'd bought some wonderful souvenirs in the Plaka, lunched on dolmades and tzasiki in little outdoor restaurants with real grapes hanging from the vines on overhead trellises, been through museums, seen hundreds of statues and icons and found one of the best McDonalds she'd ever seen. Even Maggie was impressed by the marble everywhere in the ladies' room. Grand had protested eating at a "fast-food joint" but the salad bar won her over because of the abundance of feta cheese and Calamata olives. Frankly it was all becoming a blur. Grand had made it all very interesting by working in the stories of Greek myths whenever she could. But Jennifer was disappointed in one thing.

That was why she was looking forward to Sam's arrival so much. She felt a little guilty about that. She was looking forward to seeing Sam, of course, but mostly she was looking forward to Sam taking Maggie out of the picture. It was very frustrating. From the moment she'd met them at the plane in Vancouver, until now, Jennifer had not been able to be alone with Grand long enough for them to talk. Or for Grand to talk and Jennifer to find out what it was she wanted to tell her. And not a word had been said about her father.

Had she only imagined that the promised conversation would be about her father? She tried to remember exactly what Grand had said over the phone. Something about looking forward to being alone with her, and things Grand wanted to tell her. How had she put it? "...Things that I can't really say on the phone." There'd been no mention of Dad in that conversation at all, Jennifer realized. She'd been dreaming about being the one person Grand would talk to about Dad's whereabouts, and it might not be that at all. It made her chest feel tight and she swallowed hard and turned away from where Grand and Maggie were now standing so they couldn't see her face.

Of course, she reminded herself, the mere fact that Grand wanted to talk specially to her was something unusual – amazing even. Jennifer knew that her mother often confided in and discussed things with Maggie. She wasn't supposed to know and Maggie tried not to let on, but sometimes Jennifer found out. It was part of Maggie being "the sensible one." Jennifer understood that, but it hurt anyway.

She was so preoccupied she didn't notice anything until she saw Maggie and Grand going forward to meet Sam. She surprised herself then by running ahead and giving him a hug, then caught a look from Maggie and ended up punching him in the arm. She was truly glad to see him, she realized. As if everything had been on hold and now the adventure could begin.

The chance to be alone with Grand came even sooner than she expected. The four of them went to the roof-garden restaurant at their hotel for dinner than night. It was a welcome-Sam-goodbye-Athens celebration, though they'd be spending a few days here after the cruise. That would be their chance to give Sam a special tour. Maggie was giving him a rundown of the history of the Acropolis.

"People have been living on that hill since the Stone Age...and there were temples there for a long time, even one called the pre-Parthenon. The Parthenon was built in 438 BC," Maggie recited carefully. "Actually," she laughed, it was *finished* in 438 and started in 447...I love the way time seems to go backwards when you're counting BC!"

Maggie was a goldmine of information, Jennifer thought resignedly, she'd have no trouble at all with that essay.

"And did you know that it's been everything from a Christian Church to a Moslem mosque to a storage place for gunpowder," Maggie continued. "That was during the war between the Venetians and the Turks, and a stray shell hit it and blew the roof off. Imagine, it stood for two thousand years and then got blown up!"

Jennifer groaned. There was no stopping Maggie when she got started.

"And did you know," Jennifer interrupted, "that there's even a temple...well, the ruins of one...honouring your runners, Sam?" She paused dramatically and pointed, though she really couldn't see it from there. "The Temple of Nike!"

Grandma laughed. "I'm really impressed with how much you've learned Maggie." She folded her napkin. "Jennifer," she said, getting up from the table, "I'm going to call it a day. Why don't you come with me and Maggie can continue to give Sam a condensed Acropolis tour." Grandma winked at Jennifer behind Maggie's back as she moved away from the table.

"Right with you, Grand," she said, getting up. It was really quite funny to see the amazed expressions on Maggie's and Sam's faces. They never expected Jennifer to follow without protest or not to insist on being the last one to leave.

"The Temple is Athena Nike, Goddess of Victory," Jennifer could hear Maggie saying. She hoped Sam would survive the barrage of information.

"I hope that wasn't too obvious," Grand said as they got into the tiny elevator to go down to their room. "I do have some packing to do, and so do you." She smiled conspiratorily at Jennifer, "I believe, though, that your sister could leave at a moment's notice, she doesn't seem to have even messed up her suitcase!"

Jennifer laughed. Sometimes she felt more like kindred spirits with Grand than she did with Maggie. She couldn't wait to get to the room and hear whatever it was Grand had to tell her. But the elevator didn't stop at the 8th floor where their room was. Grand must have accidentally pushed the lobby button.

"I know, Jennifer, that I must have left you in suspense," Grand said apologetically. "And I know you've been waiting impatiently to hear what I might be going to say."

This was it! At last, Jennifer thought. "I hoped..." she said softly, "...that it was about Dad."

"Very astute, my Dear," Grand said, smiling at her. "But I'm afraid there's not much to say. It's been two years since I've heard from him. He wasn't the greatest letter writer, but he did keep in touch – postcards mostly."

Jennifer nodded. Just like Grand. Postcards from exotic places. She realized now that maybe that was why Grand hadn't phoned for such a long time. She didn't want Jennifer to ask questions about Dad. Questions she couldn't answer.

The elevator door opened into the lobby. Luckily there

was no one waiting for it. Grand pushed the button and stood facing Jennifer.

"First, of all, you should know that the reason your mother hasn't told you anything is because none of us know anything *definite* really, after he stopped flying into Dubai. We're sure about that much."

The elevator stopped again and Jennifer looked up at the numbers. 10th floor. Grand had pushed the wrong button again. Jennifer watched her this time. Strange. She was pressing the lobby button again. Hard to believe Grand playing little-kid-ride-the-elevator games. They might be kindred spirits but Jennifer had quit doing this years ago.

"Last year, I heard through a diplomat's daughter – she's a journalist and we worked together on a story in Paris once –" Grand looked a little sheepish at Jennifer's look of interest, "...no, nothing exotic, I'm afraid...a fashion show or two. Anyway, Ghislaine contacted me...nothing definite..." Grand cautioned. "Just that there were some pilots who'd been flying into Syria – three of them actually – one American, one French and one Canadian..."

The door opened to the lobby again. A couple got on. Squeezing into the tiny space with them. Jennifer watched as the man pressed the 3 button. Thank goodness. They wouldn't be on long. She squeezed back into the corner. There was a sign in the elevator: Maximum 6 Passengers. She and Maggie had wondered all week how they would ever get that many people on. She noticed that Grand had pushed the roof button this time.

Jennifer couldn't stand it, "...he's a hostage?" she blurted out as the door closed behind the couple.

Grand nodded, her eyes filled with tears, "...we don't know...anything definite. I don't know how Ghislaine found out, maybe through her father...but she used to have a good friend in Israeli intelligence.... She just told me she over-heard his name mentioned and thought she'd contact me to see if it could be..."

"But there hasn't been anything in the news about hostages in Syria!" Jennifer protested. She and Sam had been excelling in Current Events as long as there was any mention of hostages.

Grand shook her head sadly, "Maybe 'prisoner' would be a better word. 'Hostage' indicates that you can negotiate and have them freed." She reached out and pressed the 10th-floor button just in time for the elevator to stop. Grand looked out at the empty corridor and held the door open but didn't get off the elevator. "Ghislaine said she'd arrange for her friend to meet me, or meet me herself at one of our tour stops." She let the door shut again. "If it's one of the Turkish ones, it will probably be Ghislaine." Grand sighed. "It would make things much easier if we knew *where* whoever it was intended to meet us."

"But why isn't...why aren't the governments trying to do something?" Jennifer's voice was getting out of control. "Aren't they supposed to stick up for their citizens?"

Grand frowned and shook her head. "That's what we always think, isn't it? And I expect they are, but with relations the way they are with Syria and some of the other Middle Eastern countries, it's all being done through the intelligence agencies..." she looked very sad, "...if anything...."

The door opened to the roof and Grand cut off in mid-sentence. Someone was waiting for the elevator.

"Well, look at this!" Grand said brightly, rummaging through her purse. "I didn't leave my glasses in the restaurant after all! I've dragged you up here for nothing." She nodded to the man getting on the elevator and pressed the button for the 8th floor.

Obviously, that was the end of the elevator ride. Jennifer recognized the man. Not much taller than Grand, he was dark with a bushy moustache that seemed too big for his face. There was a little Harry Potter scar near his mouth that disappeared into his moustache as if it was meant to hide the mark. He was in the room just beyond theirs, so he'd be getting off at the same floor.

When they got off the elevator, the man stood back politely to let them go ahead, but Grand shook her head.

"Do go ahead!" she said, smiling in a friendly way. "These halls are so narrow and I'm afraid I've slowed down with all the walking we've been doing." She put her hand on Jennifer's shoulder and leaned heavily as she hobbled aside to let the man pass.

Hah! thought Jennifer, almost smiling, Grand had been holding her own with them all week. "I may be sixty," she'd say, "but I can still leap small buildings at a single bound!"

The man moved reluctantly by as Grand held Jennifer back to her side, moving at a snail's pace. Jennifer thought perhaps the hobble was too exaggerated to be believed, but it worked. The man had no choice but to go on down the hall. He stood at the door, taking a long time to find his key.

Even more unusual than the walk was the tone of voice Grand was now using to speak to Jennifer.

"And I don't want to hear another word about this," she scolded loudly, "Not a single word, young lady."

Sam tried to hide a yawn and failed.

Maggie laughed apologetically. "I *have* been boring you. And keeping you up, after flying all that way." She pushed back her chair and got up. Grand had left a tip before she went, all Maggie had to do was sign her name and write the room number on the bill. She nodded to the waiter as she left. It all made her feel very sophisticated like an international movie star.

They waited a minute for the elevator and then decided to take the stairs nearby. They arrived at their floor laughing and breathless.

"Have you ever been on a real ship before?" Sam asked.

"Only in books," Maggie laughed. "It is going to be sooo great."

She heard the elevator door open and turned to see the man from the restaurant enter the hallway and come towards them. Sam's room came first, then hers with Jen and Grand, and she knew the man was just beyond them. He's been coming and going all week, she thought, like a tourist, but I never see him loaded down with bags of shopping or guidebooks the way we always are. She had seen him with a camera once, though, when they'd run into him at the restaurant below the Acropolis. He'd been taking pictures of it at sunset. Jennifer had waited until he left and then tried one from the same spot, but the picture hadn't turned out at all, the Acropolis didn't even show up. Of course, he probably had a much better camera or he'd shot at a different angle or something.

"See you in the morning," she said as Sam unlocked his door. She had to knock and wait for Jennifer or Grand she'd forgotten to get the extra key from Grand.

The room was a mess of packing. Maggie stared. If she was lucky, she could shove the piles of Jen's clothes over so that there'd be room for her to climb into the bed they shared.

"Organized disorder," Grand laughed. Her bed wasn't much better, Maggie noticed.

"I'll have this stuff out of the way in a jiff," Jennifer said, grabbing an armful of clothes and trying to cram them into a suitcase already stuffed with souvenirs and hats.

"Sure you will!" Maggie said shaking her head in disbelief. "Never mind, I'm going to take a bath." It would be rather a treat, she thought, the first time all week when the shower/bath enclosure wasn't draped with her sister's laundry dripping all over her.

She used a whole package of bubble bath to celebrate and then lay back. She could hear Jennifer's frequent outbursts of, "Grand, have you seen my...?" followed by a yell of, "Maggie! did you take my..." And then more quietly, "oh here it is." But mostly it was the most peaceful time she'd had since they arrived. It gave her time to think and to wonder.

She'd been glad to see Sam because he was fun and she liked him, but also, she had to admit, because he could keep Jennifer occupied so that she'd have a chance to talk to Grand alone.

Just before she left Mum had taken her aside, looking worried. "I hope your grandmother hasn't got some ulterior motive for this trip...I mean, it seems strange to be travelling to that part of the world and taking you two along."

Maggie was amazed. She thinks Grand knows something about Dad. The thought hadn't occurred to her. Had it occurred to Jennifer? Maggie didn't need two guesses – true or not, it was just the sort of thing that would. She tried not to let her suspicions show in her face. She might as well not have bothered. Mum knew Jennifer only too well.

"I don't want Jennifer getting a bee in her bonnet and deciding to pull some stupid detective thing. Greece and Turkey aren't that far from the Arab Emirates...." Her mother had then looked miserable, "it makes me wish you weren't going."

"Too late!" Maggie had said quickly. She was thanking her lucky stars Mum hadn't thought of this sooner – she might have decided to cancel the whole trip.

Maggie pulled the plug and reached for the bathtowel. She was sure Mum's suspicions were unfounded, but it would be good to have time to talk to Grand.

Jennifer stood at the rail of the Stella Solaris. They were just entering the harbour at Mykonos. No, not the harbour exactly. The ship was to anchor out here and everyone would get into the tender boats that came out from the harbour, and then be taken ashore that way.

She felt badly about lying to Grand. She shouldn't have said that she wasn't feeling well and didn't think she'd go ashore this time. Now Grand was feeling guilty about leaving Jennifer behind. In fact it had taken some persuading to get her to go with Sam and Maggie. Right now they were lined up down below, waiting to board the boats that were coming alongside the ship. Jennifer leaned over; she wanted to make sure that they were safely on before she proceeded with her next step.

Watching the waves below and the small craft rising and falling with the swells wasn't helping her feeling of nausea. Luckily, it didn't last long. And, at least, she consoled herself, the lie to Grand wasn't a lie anymore. She checked the deck behind her once more, to make sure that there was no one there. She knew she shouldn't risk being out in the open like this, but until she was sure that Grand hadn't changed her mind and stayed aboard to look after her, she wouldn't be able to carry out the plan she and Sam had devised.

Mostly, it was just to trail Professor Rossi, but Sam had suggested that she try to get a look in the locked drawer beside his bed. Each bedside chest of drawers had one drawer a passenger could lock to keep his valuables, and most people used theirs for their passports or extra traveller's cheques or jewellry. Sam claimed that the only glimpse he'd had of the Professor's drawer had been once when he'd come out of the bathroom, when the Professor had come in and didn't know that Sam was in the cabin at all.

It wasn't even that he'd seen anything suspicious. Dr. Rossi had shut the drawer too quickly for that. It was the way he'd behaved, locking it so furtively and then being abnormally jovial until Sam left.

"That's the only time there's been any sign of him using the drawer at all," Sam reported to Jennifer. "I was beginning to figure that he'd left it empty."

It was the only suspicious behaviour they'd encountered since they boarded the ship, so Jennifer figured they should investigate. Except Sam couldn't, he had to be above suspicion if anything was noticed. It had to be Jennifer while Sam was somewhere with a perfect alibi. Today was ideal. There was one hitch.

The Professor usually went ashore with everybody else, but this shore trip had no archaeological or historical tour connected to it. It was purely shopping and sightseeing, so he wasn't going. Not that it mattered, Jennifer thought, she'd be invisible anyway. Having him around might actually be an advantage. Knowing Sam was safely out of the way, he might open the drawer, which would give Jennifer a chance to see what he was hiding there.

And Jennifer had a key to the cabin. Sam had told the steward he'd accidentally dropped his overboard and got an extra key. She would make sure the Professor was safely on deck somewhere and just go down to the cabin and wait.

For a moment Jennifer wondered if she wasn't getting carried away by a silly kid's detective game. She looked over at the windmills above the harbour. The island did look inviting with the blue roofs and snowy whitewashed buildings. Maybe she was making a big mistake. She looked down and caught a glimpse of Sam moving out of sight in the tender boat. No sign of Maggie. If Grand had gone ahead Jennifer would never know if she was really going or had changed her mind. No, there she was, stepping on board. She was wearing her hair pulled up on top of her head, carrying her red sun hat – easy to see. Good. She almost waved, and then realized they couldn't see her. While she'd been standing there she'd disappeared.

She turned to take the deck stairs down to the lounge and noticed one of the stewards coming out. If she moved quickly, she could get by him into the little bar area. Opening a door herself would look strange, but this way she could check for Rossi. She and Sam had noticed that he frequently came here. He seemed to have made friends with one particular barman. At least Jennifer had seen him chatting with the man more than once.

It was a tight squeeze getting through the door before it shut behind the steward, but Jennifer made it. It took a minute for her eyes to become accustomed to the gloom but yes, there he was, perched on the stool at the far end, his dark curly head bent over his drink. He was dressed as usual in a sports jacket and tie, as if he were about to give one of his lectures. The barman was wiping the counter. Jennifer checked the room – nobody else there. She moved closer.

"Have you found out anything?" the barman was saying.

Jennifer saw that his name tag said Stavros. Even if it hadn't been for the words, Jennifer would have thought his manner was suspicious. He wasn't even looking at Rossi as he spoke. She came as close as she dared. She was tempted to climb up on the next stool, but was afraid it would squeak or turn or something.

Rossi shook his head. "For all intents and purposes, it looks like what it's supposed to be. A nice grandmother taking three young people on an educational trip. That's what Dr. Martell said it was and that's what it appears to be. The only reason to suspect otherwise could be pure coincidence. That trip she took to Mexico last year just happened to have a couple of envoys from Dubai and Qatar and other Arab Emirates travelling at the same time. Not exactly a typical vacation trip for people like that." Rossi did not look at the barman, just seemed to be talking to his drink.

Anyone glancing in here would never dream they were talking to one another, Jennifer thought, holding her breath.

"I'm sure the kid I'm rooming with, Martell's grandson, doesn't know anything. He's a funny, quiet kind of kid, doesn't say much when he's in the cabin, which is hardly at all. Seems very interested in the lectures. He's got quite a collection of books on Greek archaeology and history that his grandfather gave him, and when he is in the cabin, mostly he reads and makes notes. He's got a notebook with him all the time, but I managed to get a look at it and it's just diary stuff about the places they've seen."

Jennifer stifled a gasp. She'd better warn Sam about his notebook. Good thing they hadn't had anything to write about. Usually the notebook contained some of Sam's famous lists when he was trying to solve mysteries.

"What about the girls? The twins?" Stavros had his back to them now and was polishing glasses and stowing them away.

Rossi shook his head. "The one with the short hair, Maggie, definitely knows nothing. The other one..."

"Yeah, that one with the long hair, always wears the crazy hats..."

Jennifer's hand went unconsciously to her head. She was wearing the floppy yellow straw hat she'd got at a basket stall in the Plaka. It was not crazy, she thought indignantly, even though Maggie had claimed that it looked more like a basket than a hat.

"...I've noticed her looking at us whenever she passes through here. Really looks at you as if she's trying to figure you out."

Rossi nodded, still talking to his drink, "Yeah, if anybody other than Arnold's mother knows anything, I guess it would be her. She's one of those kids who sees too much. What was it Le Carré called them..." he mused, "...watchers?"

Jennifer did gasp this time. Rossi obviously knew something about her father, or he wouldn't be calling Grand "Arnold's mother." She held her breath. She had to remember every word of this.

Professor Rossi had turned sharply toward her at the gasping sound, spilling his drink as he did so. Stavros spun around too, scanned the room, then noticed the spilled drink and looked quizically at him. "Getting a bit sloppy?"

For an awful moment Jennifer forgot that she was invisible and safe. She had to will herself to stay still and not turn and run away.

Dr. Rossi stared straight at her. It was as if he could see her. Jennifer had to remind herself she was invisible and that he was only looking toward the sound she'd made, then his eyes darted around the empty room. At last, he turned, grabbed a napkin and started mopping at his shirt.

"I thought I heard something...somebody...right behind me."

Jennifer held her breath, backing away carefully.

Stavros concentrated on wiping the counter. "You've been on this chase too long, maybe it's just as well Brady is following the old lady today."

Rossi just gave him a look, "not much chance of her contacting Arnold or anybody else here, more likely Istanbul or Kusadasi, and I didn't want it to look as if I'm hanging around too much." He got up, "better change this shirt." He looked toward the spot Jennifer had been standing. "Could have sworn there was somebody there," he mumbled as he walked toward the door to the inner stairs.

Jennifer raced the other way. She had to beat him to the cabin. Stavros had ducked behind the bar doing something. She decided to risk opening the door to the deck, even if he noticed, he wouldn't know anything.

Reaching the cabin ahead of Rossi, she closed and locked the door behind her. She settled herself on Sam's bed mussing it enough to cover any indentation her body might make. She thought it was the safest place to be, no risking being in Rossi's way in the small cabin. The race down the stairs had made her out of breath, but luckily she managed to stop puffing before he walked into the room.

He took off the wet shirt and tossed it in the bottom drawer of the wardrobe, took out a clean one and went into the bathroom, closing the door behind him. Jennifer took advantage of that to move even further into the corner of Sam's bed, between the pillow and the wall. Sitting with her back wedged in the corner wasn't exactly comfortable, but it was, she thought, the safest place in the room. And if he opened the drawer and she leaned forward, she would have a good view of anything in it.

She didn't have long to wait. He went directly to the drawer and unlocked it. Jennifer held her breath. Wow! There some kind of electronic thing, like a tiny computer and a pack of cigarettes. Strange. She had never noticed Rossi smoking. He took out the computer thing and shut the drawer before she could get a better look. He went to the desk and sat down and began to key something in. It seemed like numbers. Jennifer risked crawling off the bed so that she could look over his shoulder. Not that she expected to learn much. It would be some kind of code.

She must have moved too close. Suddenly he spun around. "What the...!" He was staring at her, then peering around the cabin. He snapped the notebook shut. Jennifer backed away as far as she could, wedging herself between the wardrobe and the foot of Sam's bed. She couldn't risk climbing back on the bed with him looking.

He got up and began to move around the cabin. The bathroom door was open, Jennifer saw him go in and check the shower, then move back. He even opened the wardrobe doors and checked the cabin door to make sure it was locked. He stood for a very long time staring down at Sam's bed. She'd messed it quite a bit when she'd climbed off. He reached down and ran his hand across the bedspread, smoothing it. Would he notice that it was warmer in one corner, Jennifer wondered in dismay? Luckily, he didn't reach into the far corner where she'd been sitting. Now, he was lifting the mattress, reaching underneath. She hoped Sam didn't have anything hidden there. She slipped out of her hiding place just in time. Rossi was thorough, Jennifer thought admiringly, he moved in to where she had been standing and lifted the mattress at the bottom of the bed. Even pulled it out to look behind.

He finished the search and remade the bed, neatly and efficiently. Jennifer was impressed. It was exactly the way it had been when he'd come in. Not too perfect.

He'd left the little computer on the desk, closed, but she didn't dare move. She stood with her back to the door. Right now she'd had about enough detective work, but there was no way out. Not now. She was stuck here until he left.

ykonos was the first time they'd gone ashore with no organized guided tour and lecture. Sam hadn't even bothered to bring his notebook. Some of the passengers had stayed with a group who were being guided through the shops, but most had split up into groups on their own.

He and Maggie followed Grandmother Arnold through the winding cobblestoned streets. They were going up to the hill where the windmills stood. The streets were really just lanes, so narrow that you could barely have squeezed an automobile in. No one did. The only delivery vehicles were motorcycles with little two-wheeled wagons on the back and now and then a donkey with panniers on either side.

"I love this place Grand!" Maggie spun around enthusiastically.

Sam had to admit it was wonderful. There were shops along the way, but often just homes with stairs leading up to balconies where flowering vines spilled down the sides. And everything seemed so white and clean in the dazzling sunlight.

Maggie had stopped, peering in a shop window. "Look, Grand, it's a ring with Philip of Macedon's shield on it!"

Her grandmother stopped and came back to look. "So it is, Maggie. I think we ought to check that out, don't you?" Maggie was already on her way into the shop. "What about you Sam?"

He smiled at her and shook his head. "No, I want to get a picture while there are no tourists in sight!" He pulled out the new digital camera Grandad had given him. "I'll be right outside here, don't worry." He crouched down trying to angle so that he'd get a view of the stairs with the little pots of red flowers as well as the street.

"Darn!" he muttered under his breath. Just as he'd clicked, another passenger from the ship had come around the corner, spoiling his shot of a "no-tourist" street scene.

Sam decided to stay in this position. Once the man had gone by he could get his shot. He was tucked against a doorway and not in anyone's way. He realized that it was a doorway to a church, and remembered what he'd read in one of the guidebooks – about Mykonos being an island with over three hundred and sixty churches – because so many sailors who'd been caught in storms would promise that if they survived they would build a church in gratitude. Some of them, like the one he'd seen along the shore beyond the windmills, were so tiny that only a few people could have fit inside, but the seamen had kept their promises.

Sam wished the guy from the ship would get moving. He was coming up the street, glancing in shop windows but not going in, as if he was looking for somebody. Sam kept looking through the viewfinder. The man was still in his way, and his leg was beginning to cramp, he'd have to stand up in a minute. Luckily, when the fellow started to go into the shop, he suddenly changed his mind and moved away, on up the street. He didn't even look down at Sam. Sam waited a minute and got his picture just as one of the donkeys came around the corner. It would be even better than he'd hoped.

He'd just straightened up when Maggie came out of the shop and poked her hand at him, to show off her new ring with its sunburst insignia. "And," she said, "we got earrings for Mum with the same design!"

"It's called the shield of Vergina," her grandmother said, "I'm sure we'll see more of that sign when we get to Macedonia and Philip's tomb."

"I might do my essay on Philip of Macedon and Alexander the Great," Maggie said enthusiastically. "I could title it 'One of Histories Greatest Father and Son Teams' or something like that."

Sam followed her up the winding street. It was interesting to see Maggie acting so Jennifer-like. Usually, she would hang back when Jennifer got excited. Now she was actually skipping over the uneven stones. It was as if, he thought, there was just so much emotion between the two of them, and when Jennifer was around she used it all and there was none left for Maggie. Come to think of it, it went the other way too. When Maggie wasn't around, Jennifer could actually be sensible and serious at times. He wondered how Jennifer was doing just now. He hoped that she didn't get into trouble, although, being Jennifer, he was sure that she could figure a way out of it if she did.

"We're not far from the Maritime Museum," Grandma announced as they walked on. "Would you like to see it?"

Maggie laughed. "Can't go a day without a museum...can you Grand!" She turned to Sam, "Grand's an old sailor type, you know, there's no keeping her away from anything to do with the sea!"

"I wouldn't consider myself in that league, Dear...a raft trip or two, and one sailboat experience, do not a sailor make!" She chuckled, "but I have to admit that, for a person born and brought up on the Prairies, I've always been fascinated by ships and the people who sailed them." She turned at the next bend in the winding street. "...And I have to confess to loving museums. Wonderful to see how people lived long ago, all the things that shaped the way we live today. Anyway I think you two will like this one."

They did. It really was quite small, but it was bright and neat with interesting relics and pictures of ancient sea battles. Easy to look at, too; it seemed from the whiteness of the walls that the glorious sun of Mykonos had been brought indoors.

It was the backyard, though, that Sam liked the best. Cannons from ancient wrecks that you could touch and even climb on for pictures, and a lovely little lighthouse. He and Maggie took turns climbing up inside and taking pictures of each other leaning on the railing.

"Imagine," Grand said as they left, "living in a lighthouse... I think that would be lovely. People did – whole families – I suppose it must have been lonely and dangerous...not seeing anyone else for months at a time...."

"Sounds romantic, Grand," Maggie teased, "but what if one of your kids got sick, in the days when you couldn't radio for help. That would be scary!"

Aha! thought Sam. This was more like Maggie – Jennifer would be finding a lighthouse and moving in about now, if she'd heard this.

Grand grabbed Maggie and gave her a hug. "You are a practical Muggins," she laughed and started singing, "Oh my father was the keeper of the Eddystone Light...."

Sam and Maggie tried to sing along, even though they didn't know the words. They did manage to catch on to the chorus quite well.

"Yo ho ho! The wind blows free," sang Sam, hoping he was somewhere near the right tune, "Oh for a life on the rolling sea!"

It was fun, Sam thought. Fun to walk over the stones, singing merrily. One of the benefits of being with Maggie's grandmother. He couldn't imagine doing this with his parents, and definitely not with Maggie's mother.

People only looked at them and smiled. A man on the corner started singing something else in Greek and a few others joined in. This was what being joyful was about, Sam decided. Sunshine and being happy with friendly strangers in a beautiful place.

They'd left the museum just in time. A crowd of passengers from the ship was arriving with their guide. It wouldn't be nearly as nice to tour that small place with all those people. You'd be squashed and not able to see anything, Sam thought. He noticed that the man he'd seen on the street seemed to have joined the other passengers now. He must have found whoever it was he was looking for.

At last they emerged from the narrow streets. It seemed to Sam like a maze sometimes, but Grandmother Arnold seemed to know the way, she'd holidayed here before. They were on some terraced steps below the windmills now with a wonderful view of the ocean. It was amazingly blue, deep blue, with turquoise bits nearer shore. Sam thought the people must have got the idea for their blue, blue roofs from the colour of the ocean here. They wandered around a bit, then finally settled with relief at some tables on a patio by the ocean, to order cool drinks. Sam and Maggie stuck to the Coca-Cola but Grandmother Arnold – Sam had been told to call her Grand, but it just seemed too informal and familiar to be comfortable – was having retsina. "When in Greece, do as the Greeks do," she laughed.

"I'm sorry Jen is missing this," Maggie said.

Her grandmother frowned. "Yes, I do feel guilty about leaving her behind. It's been a lovely afternoon, a shame she didn't feel up to coming. I wonder how she's doing, I do hope she's alright."

Sam caught Maggie's eye. He could tell she was wondering too. He glanced at his watch, they'd been gone nearly four hours. Unless Jennifer had laughed, this would be the longest she'd ever been invisible. They'd never tested it to see if it just wore off by itself eventually. He wished now that they had.

Grandmother Arnold was looking at her watch, too. "Well, my dears, it's almost time to start back down to the harbour and catch one of the boats. You know, I have to confess that it's been rather nice not to be surrounded by our fellow passengers for once...I don't think I've seen one for the last two or three hours."

"Except for that man over there," Maggie pointed.

Sam was amazed. He hadn't even noticed the man before. It was the one who'd spoiled his street scene, and he was sitting at a table by the window of the place across from them. Spiros Taverna had blue chairs with tables outside, right down to the sea, and that's all he'd noticed, not the tables inside. As soon as Maggie pointed, though, the man put down his drink, got up and disappeared. Probably going to the washroom, Sam thought, but even so it was a little unnerving the way he was able to do it so quickly.

Jennifer had been watching the tender boats bringing passengers back to the ship for at least a half an hour. She was not in a good mood.

All her life she had dreamed of the exciting life of a spy or a detective, but the last two hours she'd spent trapped in the cabin with Professor Rossi had been the most totally boring of her whole life. No, she had to admit the first half-hour had been exciting and, she had to admit, frequently scary, as she'd dodged about the cabin trying to keep out of his way. But then he'd locked up the notebook, lain down on his bed and taken a nap. There was nothing for Jennifer to do but stand around waiting for him to wake up and open the door so that she could leave. She'd even have risked opening the door herself, hoping to slip out quietly, she was so desperate, but he seemed to be one of those people her mother called a "light sleeper." She'd bumped against the desk ever so softly once, and he was awake and sitting up looking around instantly. She hadn't dared move or breathe until he lay back down.

So she was cranky and tired and, of course, still invisible. Laughing was all very well as a way of reversing the spell, but she hadn't found anything funny. She'd really have to get some cartoon books or something to use when she was alone like this.

Thank goodness, there they were on the boat just pulling alongside the ship. She turned to head down to the lowest deck where they were coming on board. She'd have to get Maggie or Sam alone and figure out a way to cover for her until she could become visible again.

It took her awhile to locate them. Maggie and Grand were almost at the cabin when she caught up to them.

"What do you think it means, Grand?" Maggie was saying. "The ticket? The one I found shoved under the cabin door?"

Grand stopped so suddenly Jennifer nearly ran into Maggie. She looked up and down the hallway. She shook her head. "Honestly, Maggie, I am completely confused by it. But there are some things you should probably know. In fact, I think it's time we *all* had a talk. Tell Sam to meet us in the Game Room at five-thirty. There's hardly ever anyone there." She moved along toward their cabin. "I hope Jennifer's feeling better, the rest probably did her good," she said as she opened the cabin door.

Jennifer followed Maggie as closely as she could, slipping inside the cabin just before the door shut.

"That's strange!" Grand sounded worried. "She's not here!"

"She'll turn up, don't worry," Maggie consoled her grandmother. "Mind if I use the bathroom first?"

Jennifer slipped inside ahead of her. As soon as Maggie had shut the door Jen turned on the sink tap and clamped her hand over her sister's mouth. She could see Maggie, wide-eyed, staring in the mirror as realization dawned.

"You've got to cover for me until I can get visible again!" Jennifer whispered.

Maggie nodded. So Jennifer took her hand away. She was sorry she had. Maggie was wearing her old, disgusted, you-are-the-worst-sister-in-the-world look. "And get out of here as soon as you can, we've got to find Sam."

"Well, that's easy, I've got to give him a message."

"I heard," Jennifer growled. "What's that all about?"

"A letter...not exactly...something I found yesterday..." Maggie whispered. "Never mind...you'll find out...shhhhh."

She opened the door and they went out into the cabin. Grandma was rummaging through her suitcase. She stopped and pointed to a sweater folded carefully in Maggie's, it had a badly unravelled sleeve.

"Maggie, dear, I've never seen you wear that?" She looked a little embarrassed." "I don't suppose...I could..."

Maggie looked sheepish. "I only brought it along so Mum wouldn't find out I'd wrecked the sleeve. I was kind of hoping it would fall overboard, I guess."

"Perfect!" said Grand looking pleased, "I'll get you another sweater, if you let me have it...I'm afraid you won't get this one back!"

"No problem, Grand." Maggie opened the door. "I'll just go find Jennifer and Sam and see you later in the..."

Grandma looked alarmed. She was shaking her head from side to side. "Yes dear, I'll see you later," she pushed Maggie out of the door, "Run along now!"

Maggie stood looked back at the door Grand had quickly closed behind her. "What was that all about?"

"Never mind...Miss Know-it-all," said Jennifer smugly, *"you'll* find out. Now let's go find Sam."

He wasn't hard to find. In fact he was coming up the stairs to their deck when they reached the elevator. There was nobody else there, so when he asked Maggie, "Where's Jennifer?" Jennifer just punched him.

"Oh, I get it," he said matter-of-factly, rubbing his arm. "I get it...she's not back yet."

"No," said Maggie drily. "But she'd better be soon. We're supposed to meet Grand in five minutes in the..."

She was interrupted by Jennifer punching her and hissing in her ear, "somebody's coming," just as Professor Rossi came up the stairs. He nodded to them as he went by.

"Good evening, Dr. Rossi," Sam said politely. "Come on Maggie," he grabbed her arm and turned her back toward the cabin. "Let's go find Jennifer."

They waited for a minute to let him finish going up.

"Alright," said Jennifer. "Maggie, you go and wait for Grand. Sam and I will find a quiet place on the deck, and..." she threatened, "he will make me laugh...or else! And then we'll meet you."

Sam groaned. "It's nearly impossible to make you laugh when you're this cranky...I mean," he corrected as Jennifer punched him again, "...when you're in this mood."

He was right. When they finally gave up and went to the Game Room at quarter to six, Jennifer was still invisible.

Grand was sitting, knitting, in a cosy chair that was turned just enough, Jennifer realized, so that she could see anyone coming down the hall. Maggie had set out the Scrabble board ready, obviously, for Jennifer and Sam to play, and had curled up in another of the big chairs with a book. Very nice, Jennifer thought. Anyone looking in would think it was just a peaceful family scene.

"Ahh, there you are at last Sam, but where's Jennifer?" Grand looked worried.

Sam looked at Maggie and shrugged. "She had to go back to the room...wanted to get something," he explained.

"A cartoon book, I hope?" suggested Maggie.

Sam gave her a hopeless look. They'd better stop the hints, Jennifer thought, Grand will get suspicious. But Grand seemed to be frowning at the knitting. Funny. Jennifer had never seen Grand knit before. Obviously she wasn't very good at it, every now and then she'd jab herself with a knitting needle and cuss softly. Jennifer moved closer. That was what had happened to Maggie's sweater. Grand had taken it apart, unravelled a bit and poked the needles through. And those weren't knitting needles, much too sharp. Grand poked herself again. Some domestic scene. Jennifer started to giggle. She caught herself and moved over beside Maggie. Even Sam and Maggie looked startled at the sound. Grand jumped, jabbed herself again and said, "Blast it!" as she sucked her finger and looked around.

It was too much. Jennifer bit her lip. For a person who had spent the last twenty minutes trying to force herself to laugh and thinking she would never laugh again, she was now in the opposite boat. This was not going to be a giggle. She tried desperately to hold her breath. It came out as a snort followed by loud choking, gasping laughter that wouldn't be stifled. She poked Maggie belatedly. Maybe Maggie would be quick enough to fake it. Maggie tried. But there was no way her weak attempt at laughter or her pained expression could match the gales of laughter Jennifer couldn't control.

"Jennifer!" Grand tossed her phony knitting aside and started looking behind the chairs. There were only the few in the middle of the room, the rest were against the walls. Not really a place to hide. She stood bewildered, "Jennifer? Where is she?"

Jennifer was holding her sides, aching with laughter. Maggie had completely given up any pretense at trying to look as if she was doing the laughing, and just sat looking miserable. Sam looked terminally embarrassed. Neither of them dared look at Grand. They were looking at the floor where Jennifer stood. She'd been laughing so hard that she'd hardly noticed that her feet and hands were tingling. Luckily, Grand had her back to them checking behind the curtains that covered the window looking onto the lower deck. Jennifer's laughter died and she got out the door as quickly as she could.

She stood flat against the wall. From here, Sam could see her but her grandmother couldn't. She felt utterly miserable and not a bit like laughing now. If only it would hurry. She had feet and arms and a body now, but her face was always the last thing. She stepped forward tentatively and saw Sam shake his head violently and she pulled back as Grand finished her curtain search and came back to her chair.

"All right, Jennifer!" she called, picking up her knitting. "I give up. You're home free, if that's what you're playing!"

At a nod from Sam, Jennifer stepped around the door.

"Sorry, Grand!" she said feeling a bit ashamed. "I was going to surprise..." Jennifer stopped, she'd been about to explain that she had hidden ahead of time to scare them when she realized that might just be enough of a lie to make her invisible again. "...Well, I just couldn't handle it when I saw you with that phony knitting. Where did you get those things!"

Grand grinned. "Stopped by the kitchen and luckily shish kebab is on the menu tonight." She made a face at the fake knitting. "Skewers *look like knitting needles.* Appearance is everything in this case. So fake that Scrabble game you two, we've got some serious talking to do."

Grandmother Arnold gave them the explanation she'd given Jennifer at the hotel in Athens. Sam already knew most of it second-hand from Jennifer. He'd always liked the girls' grandmother, and he'd looked forward to this trip, but this was amazing. Better than anything he and Jennifer could have dreamed up.

"And so," she said, poking away at her knitting, Sam wondered how she'd ever got so much done, she seemed so awkward at it, "we must be very careful what we say to each other when there's anyone around. And perhaps I'm overreacting but, on the off chance the cabin is bugged, we'll be careful what we say there. That's why I shushed you this afternoon, Maggie my dear. Darn!" she said as she jabbed herself with the knitting. "You see," she continued, "we really don't have anything to go on. We just have to wait until Ghislaine or someone makes contact and we don't even know where that will be...unless the ticket means something." She turned to Maggie, "tell them, Dear."

Sam stared at Maggie. This was all news to him. Even Jennifer, who'd begun laughing at her grandmother's knitting again, stopped and said, "Okay, Muggins tell!"

"We got this ticket...an entrance ticket for Knossos." Maggie began. They listened as she explained, then he and Jennifer examined the ticket carefully. On the front was a picture labelled "Palace of Knossos, Throne Room, 1450-1400 BC" in Greek and English, the price in Eurodollars and, also in two languages, the words, "You are requested to preserve your ticket until you leave the Museum Site." The back of it was blank. It had been folded and the edges were a bit dog-eared. Nothing there that Sam could see. A picture of the throne and a wall mural behind it of some creatures that looked like sphinxes with rooster heads.

"Who was it addressed to?" he asked.

"No one. No name. Except the ship's, in the return corner. Just a plain envelope...the kind they have at the writing desk in the library...." Maggie shrugged, "...I checked."

"Maybe," said Sam to Grandma, "it's from your friend, letting you know where she'll meet you."

"It's true that she was very circumspect about phoning me. Just a casual call asking how I was and enquiring about my son. That aroused my suspicions a little and then she just told me to call soon. She didn't say anything until I phoned her back, and not until she made sure I wasn't calling from home. Then she just wanted to know the details of the cruise." Grandma Arnold shook her head. "How did the ticket get on board? I checked with our steward and no one gave it to him to deliver." She got up and moved quietly to the door to look down the hall. "I think we should take turns checking that every now and then." She sat down. "Maybe I'm just being a foolish, paranoid, old woman, but..."

"You're not, Grand!" Jennifer blurted. Sam could tell, sitting across from her, that she'd been bursting to say something ever since they'd begun. So she had found out something this afternoon. They'd been so busy trying to get her to laugh, he hadn't had time to find out.

"I guess I owe you an apology Grand," she began. "I wasn't sick this afternoon, I...I...wanted to investigate something...."

Maggie groaned. "Here, we go again!"

Obviously, Jennifer wasn't doing this very well. Sam decided to help. "It was kind of my fault, Grandmother Arnold," he explained. "I thought Dr. Rossi was acting suspicious...."

"You were right, Sam...and so is Grand..." Jennifer began. "Dr. Rossi is following you."

"Ouch!" said her grandmother, dropping the knitting entirely and staring at Jennifer.

"I overheard him talking to that barman, Stavros, this afternoon." Jennifer glanced at Sam, "I hid in the lounge...he knows something about Dad because he called you 'Arnold's mother' and said you probably were the only one who knew anything and would make contact..."

Grand nodded at Sam and he slipped quietly to the door and looked out. Nobody there.

"Jennifer," she said quietly. "Can you tell me the exact words."

Jennifer nodded and began. Sam was impressed. She was reciting carefully. Acting out the conversation. He was shocked to hear that Rossi had actually looked in his notebook. Jennifer had stopped at that point and said to him. "Good thing you hadn't written anything about how suspicious he was."

"So," said Grandmother thoughtfully when Jennifer paused after reciting the bit about making contact, "there are two of them on the ship. Stavros and Dr. Rossi..."

"Three," said Jennifer, "there's Brady...No! Maybe four. Somebody named 'Lee Carry' – at least it sounded like that. He must be on the ship because he said I was 'a watcher.' So I guess he saw me or something."

Grandmother smiled. "'Lee Carry'? 'A watcher'? No, I don't think he's on the ship. It sounds to me as if Dr. Rossi was just quoting from *Tinker, Tailor, Soldier, Spy.*"

Sam recognized that title. "Ohhh..." he said, as the light dawned, "that's a book by John Le Carré!"

Grandmother nodded. "But what about this Brady person?"

"Dr. Rossi said he was ashore this afternoon following you."

Maggie had just come back from checking the hall. "Of course!" she exclaimed, sitting down again. "The passenger in the restaurant...I think I caught a glimpse of him at the museum too! That must be Brady!"

"You saw him?"

Maggie frowned. "But he was so far away, I couldn't see him very well."

Jennifer turned towards Sam. "What about you? Can you describe him?"

Sam felt that at last he was going to be able to contribute something. He'd been beginning to feel very left out. Grandmother Arnold had all that preliminary information, Maggie had the ticket, and Jennifer had really been able to provide some amazing news. "I can do better than that," he said proudly patting the camera case.

"I believe I've got a picture of Mr. Brady." He was enjoying their shocked looks. He went on to explain about the spoiled picture of the street scene he'd taken while Maggie and Grandmother Arnold were in the shop. "If I'd have had time, I'd have deleted it, but I was in a hurry and was going to look at the pictures later and make prints of the good ones on the little photo-printer attachment Grandad gave me." He poked at the buttons on the camera "Here it is!" He held up the camera so they could see the picture of the ruined street scene. The man was wearing sunglasses and a canvas hat. "Too bad he's got his hat pulled down and the glasses, but the beard is clear...and he's wearing that blue shirt. It's definitely the same guy Maggie spotted in the restaurant. And I saw him when we were coming out of the Maritime Museum, too. I just thought he was one of the passengers going on the tour."

Grand put down the camera and beamed at them. "Wonderful!" she said, handing it back to Sam. "Make me a print and we'll see if we recognize him. I feel as if I've got the MI5 or the CIA working for me with you three." She was serious now. "But be careful with your pictures and your camera Sam. I wouldn't leave any of that equipment in the cabin where Dr. Rossi might look at it. And Jennifer Dear.." She frowned suddenly. "I'm a bit concerned about you taking such chances...please be careful." She got up to go to the door, giving Jennifer a hug on the way. "I suppose, all this checking the hall isn't necessary," she said coming back to her chair. "But I can't get over how Jennifer could have got down the hall without me seeing her!"

Sam looked at Maggie. They'd been doing all this checking for nothing. There was no way anyone would have seen Jennifer come down the hall.

"And that was all you heard?" Grandmother tossed the knitting aside.

"Yes," said Jennifer looking hard at Sam. "That was all I heard."

Sam got the picture. Nice work Jennifer. Not a lie. All she'd *heard*, but not all she'd *seen*, he was sure. She couldn't very well tell her grandmother if she'd gone into the cabin, but she must have done so. She was giving him a have-I-got-stuff-to-tell-you look just now. He hoped Grandmother Arnold didn't notice.

No. She looked to be deep in thought. He searched her face and tried to read her expression. Suddenly her face changed. There's been a tension about her ever since the trip began, Sam thought, even though she'd acted calm enough and seemed to be enjoying herself with them. Now she had a look of relief, almost joy.

"You realize why I made you repeat what Dr. Rossi said – the bit about me making contact – over and over, don't you Jennifer?"

Jennifer shook her head. Sam was puzzled too. Grandmother had made quite an issue of Jennifer being sure she was repeating Dr. Rossi's exact words about that.

"It's the best news we've had so far. If whatever intelligence agency Dr. Rossi is working for thinks that I might be contacting your father...it means they know he's alive...but they don't know where he is. It means," her voice had a catch in it but she was smiling, "that he's definitely been released or escaped!"

"Jennifer, you are completely and utterly mad!" Maggie rolled over on her stomach on the deck chair and faced her sister.

They'd arranged the deck chairs so that the three of them could talk casually. Maggie had her book, of course. Sam was sitting on the foot of Jennifer's chair with a deck of cards. They were absently playing crazy eights countdown, and whenever another passenger passed by they would begin to argue about the rules. Luckily the area was deserted. Maggie had discovered it. It was perfect because they could see anyone coming close on the deck above and they could also see whoever was on the deck below.

It was the first time they'd had together since last night. After the session in the card room they'd gone for dinner – Grand had been able to switch them to a late seating by using the excuse of Jennifer being sick. By the time they'd finished eating it had been time for bed. Maggie'd felt a little strange in their cabin now, knowing that somebody might be listening to them, but Jennifer had managed to chatter away as usual to Grand, so it was alright.

Now Jennifer had just finished telling them about following Dr. Rossi into the cabin and dodging around all afternoon.

"Oh, don't worry about me, Maggie. It's all in a days work for J. Arnold, Superspy!" She kicked Sam lightly, "Your turn!"

"Dr. Rossi was very casual about asking me why we'd all missed supper," he said, slapping down a card. "He knew we were back from the tour because he saw us at the elevator." Sam grinned. "Obviously, they lost track of all of us, just assuming we'd show up at the usual time for dinner."

Maggie looked at him admiringly. "I'd have been a bit nervous being there with him, now that you know...well, now that we know..." Actually Maggie realized they still didn't know very much. Though they knew a good deal more now that Jennifer had described what had gone on in the cabin.

"Well," said Sam, "Jennifer said that they don't suspect me. Or you. Just Grand and Jennifer."

"I," said Jennifer proudly, "am a 'Watcher'...whatever that really is. I'm going to read that book first chance I get."

"Funny, isn't it?" mused Maggie. "A spy who reads spy books? I didn't think detectives read detective books."

"Of course they do!" said Jennifer. "Don't we, Sam?"

"All the time!"

Maggie ignored them. This was serious and even if they didn't act it, she knew both Sam and Jennifer knew it too. Jennifer had lain awake beside her for a long time after they'd turned out the lights last night. Both of them pretending they didn't notice the other was awake. Maggie was willing to bet they were both thinking about the same thing. Where was their father? And why were Rossi and the others so anxious to find him?

"I wish," she said suddenly, "that we could tell Grand all that other stuff you found out, Jen. About the computer thing and the code and whatever is in Dr. Rossi's drawer."

"Believe me, Muggins, so do I. But there is no way to do it without telling her I was invisible. How do you tell your Grandmother you are able to become invisible?"

"She almost found out last night," Sam said. "We've got to figure out a way to make you laugh on cue."

Jennifer giggled, "Maybe we can get Grand to keep her so-called knitting handy!"

"Passenger approaching from the port side," warned Maggie. She'd caught a glimpse of someone coming up the stairs from the lower deck.

"Your turn!" said Jennifer quickly giving Sam another kick.

Sam slapped down a card. "Am I sevens or sixes now?"

Maggie craned her head as the man moved out of sight. He looked familiar.

Sam looked at her and nodded. "Brady," he said softly. "Same sunglasses, same crepe-soled canvas shoes.

Jennifer sat up straighter, kicking Sam out of the way to get a better look. "Rats!" she said petulantly, "I missed him!"

"Listen, Jennifer," Sam said, picking himself up off the deck, "if you don't stop kicking me...I...I'm going to tickle your feet!"

"You can't," Jennifer said, sticking her foot out towards him. "I'm not ticklish."

"Yeah, right!" said Maggie, rolling over to watch. She was glad that Sam was going to get even at last.

He grabbed Jennifer's ankle and began to tickle the sole of her foot. Maggie had to hand it to her, she'd taken a deep breath and was concentrating on her cards. It took at least ten seconds before she flipped her foot away and exploded in giggles.

"Let me try that," Maggie said grabbing her other foot. "Settle down, Jennifer, this is scientific research." Again Jennifer tried, resisted for a little while, and burst out with a paroxysm of laughter. "Aha!" said Maggie, "By Jove, we've got it. We can make her laugh on cue." She rubbed her wrist, thoughtfully, "Of course it would be even better if she didn't kick like a horse when she finally lets go and laughs."

"That'll be your problem," Jennifer gave Maggie her fiendish-sister smile. "Still, it's a relief. I'd like to check out our friend Rossi. He was parked in the bar with Stavros when I came down here." She looked at her watch. "We don't go ashore on Santorini until after lunch."

"Not so fast, there's still the problem of finding her foot when she's invisible," Sam ignored Jennifer and spoke to Maggie.

"Of course it's impossible if she doesn't co-operate." Maggie smoothed a fresh coat of suntan lotion on her legs. "She'll just have to let us grab an ankle like she did just now." She waved the bottle in Jennifer's face. "You'd better use some of this." Jennifer was starting to look a bit pinkish in spite of her tan. It wasn't like at home where the sun baked you and you felt hot before you burned, here the ocean breeze kept you cool and you didn't notice until it was too late. "It's better than yours – it's a 40 sunblock."

"Jennifer! You cheated when you shuffled the pack." Sam protested. "You couldn't possibly get all the deuces!"

"I did not!"

Maggie looked over. Jennifer sounded sincere but it was a Jennifer type of trick. Let Sam handle it, she thought, pulling her sun hat over her face. She felt lovely and drowsy, the drone of the ship, even the sound of Sam and Jennifer arguing – they'd fought about this so often before, they seemed just to be reciting words to Maggie – were just enough to let the motion of the ship rock her to sleep. She hadn't slept very well last night. She was just in the midst of that lovely drifting-down-through-fluffy-clouds feeling when she was shaken hard, so hard she nearly fell off the chaise. Shipwreck? She jerked awake and groaned. No, not a shipwreck, of course. Just Jennifer. "One of these days," Maggie made a fist.

Jennifer was looking quite pale beneath her tan. She shook her head. "No listen, I'm going to disappear for a little while, I'll meet you two in an hour in the game room." She hauled herself to her feet a bit unsteadily. "Be there!" she threatened and stumbled inside.

"What's she up to now?" Maggie mumbled to Sam. The light gradually dawned. She groaned again. "Oh, oh, she did say 'disappear' didn't she?"

Sam nodded. He was sprawled out on the deck chair laying out the cards for solitaire.

"But how?"

Sam grinned at her. "She cheated, of course!"

Jennifer ducked into the first washroom she could find. She went into a cubicle and leaned her face against the cool door. She hated this sick feeling, but luckily it was disappearing already. And so was she. Maybe she'd been a bit too impulsive about this. A little planning would be in order next time. For instance, arranging for Sam to go to the cabin sometime when Dr. Rossi was there and then leave, so that she could watch in case he opened the drawer again. Then after about an hour, Sam could come back pretending to get something he'd forgotten and leave again, letting her slip out with him.

She wished there was some way she could "borrow" that computer thing but it wouldn't work. She knew from experience that anything she picked up when she was invisible was visible. Of course, she thought, anything she had when she became invisible, her clothes, things in her pockets, even keys she was holding, went with her. Too bad she couldn't be holding the computer and it would disappear. Then she could get it out of there. But that was hopeless.

Must be about done, she thought, unlocking the door. She glanced in the empty mirror as she went by just to check.

Professor Rossi was still at the bar and the door was propped open so she had no trouble getting in. It had filled up since she'd come through before. Several couples quietly talking at tables by the windows. A noisy group of people were sitting at the other end of the bar arguing about something. There seemed to be a fairly steady stream of people walking through the lounge going to the tables out on the deck. She'd have to be careful nobody walked into her. She slipped between the bar stools not far from Rossi. Stavros was there but he was busy filling orders for the waiters. Obviously, this was not a very good time to get any information, she thought dejectedly. But just then Stavros looked over, Rossi nodded, and Stavros came towards them smiling and carrying a drink. Jennifer held her breath.

They didn't waste any time in small talk, although anybody seeing them would have assumed by their expressions that's what it was.

"You talked to Brady?" Rossi murmured.

Stavros made a very slow business of setting down the little cocktail napkin and setting the drink on it. "Yeah. Something funny." He picked up the empty glass and wiped the spotless bar slowly. "The Arnold kid – the one with the stupid hats? Wasn't with them."

Jennifer hung onto the bar and willed herself not to move. Her heart was pounding so much she was afraid they would hear it.

"Two something's funny. Where the hell did they all disappear to when they should have been having dinner?" Rossi shook his head. "And why?"

Stavros turned away and left to fill an order of drinks for one of the waiters. He returned again with a chit for Rossi to sign.

"The waiter said the kid was sick and they changed seatings," Stavros said, making a big deal out of searching the pockets of his white jacket for a pen, even though Jennifer could see one clearly. "So she didn't go ashore. Probably spent the afternoon in the cabin." Finally, he produced the pen and set it before Rossi.

Dr. Rossi shook his head. "If she was in that cabin, she is the quietest kid in the world. I listened – the bug picked up nothing from the time the door closed behind Arnold's mother and the kids before they went ashore, until the door opened when she and the other girl came back. Not a a sound." He reached slowly out and signed the chit.

Stavros shrugged. "So she's a quiet kid...or she was asleep when they left and..."

"No, her voice doesn't show up on the tape until the three of them came back to bed," Rossi sounded annoyed. "And she is definitely not a quiet kid, she could talk the Sphinx to death!" He spoke to Stavros' back as the bartender moved away. "Get Brady to watch her especially. There's no way Arnold could be on this ship, but that kid's up to something. I'll take the trip with them this afternoon, they won't give us the slip again."

Stavros was busy at the other end of the bar again. A woman who'd been sitting with the noisy people came over to sit at the bar near Jennifer.

"Oh! Professor Rossi, it's you!" she said. She had a harsh, unpleasant voice, even though she was trying to be charming. "I did want to ask you some questions about Delos..."

she started to switch bar stools to move closer to him and Jennifer barely scrambled out of the way in time.

The bar was getting more crowded all the time. Jennifer decided she might as well get out now. The woman had settled in beside Rossi and by the look of it he wouldn't have a chance to talk to Stavros again.

It's surprising, Jennifer thought as she edged her way through to the door, how hard it is to avoid having people bump into you when they can't see you. You can always edge through a crowd when you're visible, because people step aside or at least don't crash into you. Now she was seriously having to dodge, duck behind chairs, and try to keep out of the way.

She realized once she got out on the deck that she'd have to find a clock. It was a nuisance not to be able to see her watch. Luckily there was a lady sitting at one of the tables wearing one of those big Swatches. Jennifer didn't have to get too close. Almost time to meet Maggie and Sam anyway.

They were actually waiting for her by the time she got to the game room.

"Okay, you two," she said as she plopped herself down in a chair. It was still fun to see them both jump at the sound of her voice so close to them. "Grab a foot!" She kicked Maggie and laughed as Maggie made a swat at her. Sam had better luck but Jennifer was already giggling at their expressions of annoyance even before he started to tickle.

"This is pretty stupid, Jen!" Maggie was disgusted. "What's the big idea taking off like that! It's a good thing you're here early because Grand's meeting us, she wants to talk to us before we go ashore."

"Oh good, there you all are!" Grand's voice preceded her into the room. She glanced around. "Where's Jennifer? I heard her voice as I was coming along, there's no mistaking that giggle!" She shook her head as if her patience was wearing thin. "Don't tell me she's hiding again? We really don't have time for that." She looked at Sam. "Sam!" she said amazed, "What *are* you doing?"

Jennifer almost forgot herself and spoke. What on earth did Sam think he was trying to do? He still had hold of her ankle and she had to get out of here. She kicked him with her other foot, he flinched but held on. She drew back again. You asked for it! Jennifer thought grimly, preparing a kick that would knock him into the middle of next week.

"Grand," Maggie was speaking quickly, her voice urgent, "There's something we've got to tell you...about Jennifer!"

Jennifer stopped her kick midway and aimed it instead at Maggie. There was a satisfying "ooof" as her foot landed in Maggie's stomach. Luckily for Maggie the kick had lost power because Jennifer couldn't quite reach to where she was sitting.

Grand was staring at Maggie now. Maggie made a grab in vain for Jennifer's foot, missed and kept on. "She's invisible!"

"Now really, Maggie..." Grand began and then her eyes widened and she simply sat and stared.

Sam was on the floor now and appeared to be wrestling with nothing at all. No, thought Jennifer with horror as she looked. He's wrestling with a foot. My foot. It was too late for her to get out of there now.

Maggie was still valiantly trying to explain. "You see there was a spell and she tried it and she can be invisible...."

Jennifer aimed a half-hearted kick at her sister who caught her now-visible foot and hung on. It can't get much worse, she thought, ceasing to struggle. Unless, of course, their poor grandmother had a heart attack at the sight of those two busy holding onto a pair of disembodied feet.

"...And..." Maggie went on grimly, "...it always takes a little while for her to get back..." She waved Jennifer's foot, which by now had seemed to grow a leg attachment. "It's...it's just that she comes back in pieces..." she added apologetically.

Jennifer gave up and slid off the chair. She dared a look at her grandmother, who was staring in disbelief. She did look rather sickly, certainly paler than usual. "I'm alright, Grand, really I am." Thank goodness her body was coming in now, she did look silly propping herself up with only arms and legs.

"Her head always appears last," Sam said reassuringly.

"Actually, it's her face that comes last" Maggie corrected matter-of-factly.

Grand continued to stare, shaking her head slowly. Jennifer was relieved to see that her complexion was returning to something a little closer to normal. "I don't believe it," she was saying softly. "I don't believe my own eyes."

Jennifer wasn't sure if she had a face or even a mouth, she couldn't wait. "Why did you do it?" She said miserably, "why didn't you let me get out of here?"

"Don't you see, Jennifer?" Maggie was pleading to her, "we had to let Grand in on it...."

"She's got to know everything you've found out...." Sam put in earnestly.

"It's the only way!" Maggie finished.

Jennifer nodded miserably.

Grand was looking at her, still shaking her head. "If you'd told me about this I'd never have believed you." She shut her eyes and shook her head. "I probably won't even believe *myself* tomorrow." She opened her eyes and looked at Jennifer again, examining her face carefully. "There you are! All of a piece now. Thank goodness!" She looked very relieved. "Now suppose you tell me all about this from the very beginning."

It seemed to Jennifer that it would take forever, until Maggie took over and reminded them that they had less than an hour until they had to start boarding the boats to go ashore on Santorini. Then they stopped interrupting each other and let Maggie tell it. No doubt about it, Jennifer thought admiringly, all those essay outlines must have an effect, she went through the whole invisibility adventure in no time.

"So," said Grand. "You don't even have to use the spell now? When you lie you become invisible and when you laugh you are visible again." She looked at the three of them. "And you, Jennifer are the only one who used the spell?"

Jennifer glanced at Maggie sheepishly, "Actually, I persuaded Sam to try it...didn't take much persuading once I had it figured out that I could control it...but it didn't work for him at all."

"It didn't work for me either," said Maggie.

"What?" Sam and Jennifer spoke in unison. Jennifer couldn't believe her ears. Maggie the cautious had risked it? That was news. "When?"

"Never mind," said Grand, "we've got to get moving. I'd skip this trip entirely and just stay here and get this all sorted out," she turned to Jennifer, "I take it that you've more to tell me, now that I understand how you've been able to learn it...."

Suddenly Grand turned toward the doorway. Nobody had come in all the time they'd been there, but Jennifer's heart sank when she realized what Grand must be thinking. Somebody could have been in the hallway, listening all this time. Brady! Neither of them spoke and then Jennifer realized Grand was smiling and nodding at Sam. When he'd got up from the floor after Jennifer became visible, he'd taken the chair that Grand had been sitting in last night. He'd been watching the hall all this time.

"Way to go Sam!" Jennifer breathed.

"Yes, indeed!" Grand was smiling at him. "As I was saying, we have to go ashore. I don't know how I could have forgotten it, but I remember that Ghislaine used to have a friend here on Santorini...owned a restaurant. In fact I even came with her for a brief visit once...I just hope I can remember...it was so long ago." Grand stood up, "now let's get a move on. We'll have to catch up on the rest later."

Santorini was a very different type of island from Mykonos. Cliffs towered over the bay where their ship had anchored. Above them white and blue buildings clung to the edge. It was all they could see of the city of Thera.

Once ashore there was heated discussion as to how they were going to go up. Jennifer wanted to ride the donkeys but Grand thought that since there was so little time they should take the cable cars. Sam wasn't sure which one he would opt for if it was left up to him, but thought the cable cars would be fun – like the gondola ride up Whistler's Mountain in Jasper. He watched the cars moving straight up the cliff like an ungainly blue caterpillar. That would be his choice, he decided, but there was no way he was going to get into a family argument against Jennifer.

Finally Maggie asked, "How did you go up the time you came with your friend, Grand? Maybe it would be easier if you tried to retrace it exactly."

Grandmother Arnold smiled at her, "Clever Maggie! Of course! I don't think the donkeys come up at the same place.

We took the cable car that day." She turned to Jennifer. "Never mind Sweetie, you can ride down on the donkeys. You won't feel so sorry for them having to make that hard climb." She shook her head. "I just hope I can remember the way...I remember that we walked a very short way, narrow streets, down stairs and her friend's place was on a corner..." She frowned, "...something of Atlantis...Daedalus?...no... Dionysus..."

"Quick," said Sam, "let's take this one." He'd noticed that Dr. Rossi had got out of the boat behind theirs and was only a little way behind them in line. Jennifer had managed to fill him in about who was going to tail them and they had decided to try to avoid him.

It didn't work. Rossi managed to push his way ahead and was the last person on with them. Jennifer moved over to sit in the corner by Grand but Sam had to smile and act normal and sit beside Rossi.

The ride up was spectacular. Especially being able to look down on their ship sitting in the harbour. From here you could really see that this was the crater of an ancient volcano, except the ocean had filled it and left the jagged circle of rock that stuck out of the water. That circle was the island of Santorini. Near the bottom he could see some of the caves with fronts like houses that people lived in. He'd read about that in the guidebook, now he wondered what it would be like to live in the side of a cliff in a land of earthquakes.

"This is thought by some, Sam," Dr. Rossi was saying in a friendly voice, "to be what is left of the island of Thera which was destroyed by an earthquake in 1450 BC. Some people even think it might have been what started the legend of the lost continent of Atlantis...people later on...seeing the remains of buildings under the water."

"That's fascinating Dr. Rossi," Maggie was listening intently. "I like that. Have they been able to prove it? I mean modern archaeologists?"

Good old Maggie, Sam thought. He glanced at Jennifer who was squinting fiercely at Dr. Rossi. He wished she'd stop that. No wonder they think she's suspicious.

Dr. Rossi had turned and was smiling at Maggie. "I'm afraid it's still in the realm of theory. But it was definitely that same eruption that destroyed the Minoan civilization on Crete. There is a Minoan-age city they've excavated at Akrotiri on the southwestern tip of the island."

"I guess you'll be going to see that while we're here, won't you Dr. Rossi," said Jennifer brightly.

"Errrr...no," Dr. Rossi looked uncomfortable. "There isn't enough time, we've only got the afternoon...and...."

"It's a small island, it shouldn't take too long," Jennifer interrupted.

Sam wished Jennifer would cool it. No point in pushing the man. Once again, to his relief, Maggie came to the rescue.

"I can't wait to get to Crete," she said. "The Labyrinth, the Palace of Knossos...."

They had reached the top now and they waited for the doors to be opened so that they could get out.

"You know Mrs. Arnold," Dr. Rossi was waiting for Grand to climb out, "you have certainly done a wonderful thing bringing these youngsters on a trip like this."

"Thank you, Professor, I hope so," she gave Jennifer a look only Sam and Jen would catch, "it's very hard to keep up with them sometimes!"

Sam took this to mean that they should spread out and look as if they were wandering, so that they wouldn't be so easy to follow.

The group from the ship moved slowly, filling the narrow stone streets. Along one side all you could see was the ocean, with the two small volcanic islands looking lifeless in the midst of the deep blue sea. The sun was perfect so Sam lingered with some of the other tourists to try to get some pictures. It was a good excuse to see if Brady had come up in one of the other cars, but he'd have wanted to take them anyway. The sun was brilliant and the white and blue buildings dropping along the cliffside made a great shot, in fact he was sure it was almost identical to a postcard he'd seen.

He could see Grand threading her way through the crowd. Jennifer and Maggie were stopping to look in shop windows, letting her get ahead, but Dr. Rossi was walking right beside her telling her something. Probably more about the history of the place.

It looked to Sam that the only thing to do was to catch up and see if he could distract Rossi, just in case. He'd seen a sign pointing to the Archaeological Museum; it looked like he'd have to make the sacrifice of being bored for an hour or so and talk Rossi into going with him. Too bad it had to be him, Maggie might actually enjoy it. He caught up easily, Grand was making a great show of having trouble getting down some stone steps where the street dropped to another level. She moved on to a corner and stopped. Sam moved past her and could see a patio with some tables ahead. The sign along the street said Dionysus of Atlantis.

"My goodness," she said to nobody in particular. "My hip seems to be bothering me again. Even a little climbing..." she turned to Dr. Rossi, "don't let me hold you up." She moved through the archway entrance, "I'll just sit here for a little while. Perhaps a cool drink."

Jennifer propelled Maggie right on by them towards the sign. "Fine," she said quickly, grabbing Maggie's hand. "I need to use the washroom...c'mon Maggie!"

That left Sam feeling rather awkward, but if scattering was called for, he could handle it. He pointed to a shop partway down the narrow street. "That looks like a good place to get something for my mother. Tell the girls to catch up with me." He walked away without looking back, started examining some painted cushion covers and hangings with pictures of the houses on the cliffs of Santorini, on a table outside the shop, and, as soon as he could, moved around so that he could look back to see what Dr. Rossi was up to.

He got a glimpse of Grandmother Arnold getting up to move under the awnings out of the hot sun. She was sitting alone, talking to the waiter and a Greek woman sitting at the next table, who seemed to be translating. There was nobody else in the restaurant that he could see, and Rossi was nowhere in sight. Sam moved on to a stand with calendars. He picked them up to examine the pictures and look at the price. He really did want to get something for his mother. Now he could glance back again.

He made a quick scan, looking for Rossi. Not in the restaurant, he must have gone into one of the shops.

He saw Jennifer and Maggie come out a door further on, probably the inside part of the restaurant heading this way. Arguing as usual. Mostly Maggie, which struck Sam as a bit strange. Jennifer stopped at the shop across from where he was, she was turning the postcard rack, making a few selections. Oh, oh, Sam thought, he'd glimpsed some hats just inside the shop, any minute now Jennifer would be adding to her collection. But instead Maggie stopped and went in and picked up a hat. She seemed about to take off her own hat and try one on, but changed her mind and went over to a shop across the street.

The street was filling with more people from the ship. They streamed down the narrow stairs and spilled around the corner. He supposed if he was going to buy something he'd better make up his mind before the shop got too crowded. Jennifer had moved casually around him and gone inside. Good, he'd ask her advice about the calendar and see if she'd seen Rossi. He ducked in after her.

"Jennifer," he reached out to stop her and stopped in amazement. It was Jennifer's basket-turned-upside-down hat and it hid her hair and most of her face, but when she turned toward him, it was Maggie. "What...the...?" He stopped. Several people from the ship were crowding into the shop, including a man he recognized as Brady. Maggie saw him too.

"Oh those are really nice, Sam!" she said quickly. "That's what you're going to get for your mother?"

Sam nodded and moved over to get in line. "It's four Euros, that's about $6.00 Canadian." He stopped, remembering that he was supposed to be talking to Jennifer, not Maggie.

He didn't want her to give herself away by giving a lecture on the exchange rate. Jennifer didn't have the slightest idea about Greek money. If she had it, she paid it. Usually, just like at home, she was broke. Maggie started to reach in her purse and stopped. Sam knew she was going for her calculator, but of course, he realized, Jennifer and Maggie had not only switched hats and tops, but purses too. They'd both been wearing white shorts and sandals. No wonder Jennifer as Maggie hadn't been able to try on hats. She'd have her hair stuffed up inside the white sun hat Maggie'd been wearing. And with this floppy hat Maggie had on her short hair didn't show. Obviously they'd planned this switch when they'd rushed back to the cabin to change just before they came ashore. Very nicely done.

They came out of the shop and could see that Jennifer, the real Jennifer, had moved back toward the corner. He followed. Sam knew she was trying to check on Dr. Rossi. Jennifer stopped and was looking at some malachite eggs in a very posh jewellery shop, but beyond her Sam could see Dr. Rossi. He'd seated himself on a stool in the little ice cream parlour on the corner across from the restaurant patio, and was drinking something. It was close enough to the corner that he could watch anyone who came up to where Grandmother Arnold was sitting, while keeping an eye on the three of them.

"Jennifer," Sam said, grinning at Maggie, "do you remember those old comedy acts where..." he made sure they'd moved out of earshot of Brady, although he could see they were still being followed, "...where everybody keeps popping in and out of different doors? What do you say we have a little fun?"

He noticed Jennifer had disappeared into the jewellery shop.

Maggie caught on. "Right! You take that side of the street and Jennifer and I'll take the other." She headed into a candy shop nearby. Moments later Jennifer came out. Meanwhile Maggie – or was it Jennifer? – came out of the front door of the posh jeweller's shop. Sam could see Dr. Rossi looking at them.

The shops on Sam's side of the street seemed to only have one entry. But the ones on the girls' side had doors to both this street and the one beyond, so they could go in one and come quickly out the other. Sam noticed that once or twice Maggie managed to wait until Brady was about to go in one side before she came out the other. Twice Sam managed to find shops with back doors and then he could reappear much further down the street. Jennifer as Maggie had disappeared completely by now, and Sam wondered how she'd managed to find anyone to lie to, until he glanced up toward the restaurant and noticed her sitting at the table with Grand. He continued the game a bit longer, often getting around corners and out of sight of both Rossi and Brady for some time. Still he didn't want to get too far away. The streets were winding enough and all looked so much alike that he was afraid of losing his way. Finally he started moving back down the street. He and Maggie as Jennifer finally met again in the shop where they'd begun.

"I'm going to do this a little longer and then meet you with Grand." She left by one door as soon as Brady came in the other, and Sam and another passenger blocked his way for a little while so he couldn't turn around and go right back out. Sam apologized profusely and noticed with pleasure that Brady was sweating rather a lot and didn't look too happy.

"Well," said Grandmother, smiling at them, when all three had finally joined her and Maggie and Jennifer had made another trip to the washroom to become themselves again, "this has been a lovely afternoon and now perhaps we should make our way back down to the ship."

Sam knew by the emphasis on the word "lovely" that she

had something to tell them, although every time he'd been close enough to look she'd been sitting alone.

"Yes," said Jennifer, "and *Maggie* even managed to buy a hat!" She pointed to a bag Maggie was now carrying.

Maggie looked a bit surprised and then opened the bag to take a peek and recoiled slightly. "Yes," she said forcing a smile, "I just *love* purple."

"You can hang it with mine, Maggie, I know just the spot." Jennifer had decorated their cabin by arranging her hat collection on the walls with thumbtacks.

Sam waited impatiently for whatever Grandmother had to tell them, all the way down the cliff and back to the ship, because Dr. Rossi had caught up to them and stuck very close. So it was not until they met in the game room for a few minutes before supper that Grandmother Arnold managed to give them her news. The Greek woman in the café had really been Ghislaine. And it was true. James Arnold and one of the other captives, the French one, had managed to escape. The Frenchman had managed to make contact and then had disappeared.

"We think Dr. Rossi and his friends are probably with the CIA, trying to find your father and learn what he knows about the possible location of their man."

"But why?" asked Jennifer, "doesn't Dad just contact somebody? Like an embassy or something?"

Grandmother sighed. "It's not that easy. The Americans are not the only ones who are trying to find them. The Syrians are also trying to reach them..." her face was grim, "and we don't want them to find them first."

Sam stared at Jennifer. She looked as if she was going to cry. Maggie's face had become still and pale under her tan.

"We've...we've got to do something..." she breathed.

Grandmother Arnold nodded, her voice back to normal. "In two days we'll be in Istanbul. Ghislaine thought that would be the most likely place – her contact was able to let him know what ship we were on, I'm sure he'll be watching for its arrival. Jennifer, did you get the package Ghislaine left in the washroom?" She smiled at Jennifer now. "You came back just in time, my Dear. I would never have dared go in immediately after her, it would have looked too suspicious."

Jennifer nodded. "It's in Maggie's purse. Good thing I had hers, I've got so much stuff crammed into mine it would have never fit."

Maggie looked surprised, but she reached into her purse and removed a slim package. It was really no more than a large envelope, Sam thought. He watched as Grandmother opened it. Inside were two British passports and some money. He took one last look down the hall and then crowded with the others to look over Grand's shoulder. Neither passport said James Arnold, but there was a picture of him in one. Jennifer started to reach for it, but her grandmother put everything back in the envelope and stood up to leave.

"We're late for dinner already and we don't want to arouse any more suspicion. By the way," she said as the four of them went down the hall, "I'm not sure whether the game you were playing with our friends this afternoon was wise, but it was quite effective. Ghislaine was very impressed. You distracted Dr. Rossi a great deal. Enough that we were able to have a few words without him noticing."

Maggie studied the menu in the dining room carefully. She wished the ship would serve more Greek food. They seemed to have it only at lunchtime and then only one dish, and nothing interesting like the wonderful food Grand had introduced them to when they were in Athens. It was her only complaint, though, the food was really good, lots of choices and a very attentive young Greek waiter who'd help her choose something when she couldn't make up her mind.

She loved dressing up and eating out. It made her feel elegant and special. Jennifer, on the other hand, was – Maggie stared disapprovingly at her sister – hopeless. Even Grand couldn't get her to dress up properly, although the dress code in the ship's restaurant wouldn't allow her to wear shorts. Maggie even wished she'd brought more than one dress-up dress, but Grand had bought her a really nice peasant skirt, sort of gypsy looking, and she was mixing it with a few different blouses. While it didn't quite fit in with the international-sophisticate image she preferred, it did make her feel nicely exotic. Jennifer had one very like it. They never dressed alike, but they'd both liked the skirts and it didn't seem too much. Tonight Jennifer was wearing hers with a huge white T-shirt and a brightly coloured vest with little mirrors sewn on it. Actually the look wasn't bad at all, Maggie thought. Kind of funky. But then, the vest was unique. Jennifer had found it at the Plaka the first day they were in Athens and spent most of her shopping money on it. Maggie had a sudden, horrible thought.

"Jennifer! Whose money did you use to buy that hat?"

She didn't even have to wait for an answer. Of course it would be the money in the purse Jennifer'd been carrying at the time – Maggie's. Maggie began digging in her purse counting her Euros.

"Does this mean that I don't get to keep the hat?" Jennifer asked meekly.

When they got back to the cabin from Santorini Maggie had tossed the purple monstrosity to Jennifer. "It's yours," she'd said, "you know I wouldn't be caught dead in it."

But she hadn't known then whose money Jennifer had used to buy it. "Not unless you pay for it," she said grimly.

Maggie stopped counting and stared in her purse. She wasn't sure how much they could say at the table. Dr. Rossi sat at a table nearby, and although Jennifer hadn't heard anything about it being bugged; it was a possibility, since they were assigned the same table for the whole trip. They'd all agreed that discussions at the dinner table and cabin would be very circumspect, but she wasn't going to be able to stand not knowing about this. She lifted the ticket for the Palace at Knossos up just high enough to show Grand. "What about..." She was sure that Grand would understand the rest of the unspoken question. Did Ghislaine know who sent the ticket?

She waited. Both Sam and Jennifer had seen her flash the ticket, realized what it meant and were waiting too. But nobody else would. She was holding it with the Euros in her hand.

Grand folded her napkin and glanced calmly around the room. "Poor Dr. Rossi," she said nodding in his direction. "He seems to attract quite a bit of attention from various women on the ship. I see there are four sitting at his table. I suppose it's part of his job...to be charming to all the single women. But he must spend a lot of time giving extra lectures."

"Like the one we had today..." Jennifer began.

Grand nodded, "...it must be tiresome after a while...trying to explain things." She looked at Maggie and then down to the ticket she was returning to her purse. "She knows nothing." She turned to Nikos, their waiter, as he came to the table. "I suppose you are here to tempt us with the dessert selections."

Maggie closed her purse. So Ghislaine had not sent the ticket and didn't know who had. She glanced at Jennifer. She could tell by the hope in her eyes that their thoughts were alike. Practical Maggie doubted there was any way her father could have arranged for them to get the ticket. Jennifer would assume he had somehow done it – anonymously, to protect them from anyone knowing he was contacting them. Jennifer's eyes were shining with hope. Maggie wished she could believe as well. In spite of her doubts she didn't want to quench the wonderful, shining feeling that grew inside her.

Tomorrow they would spend the day in Crete, tomorrow they would see the Palace of Knossos and hear the stories of

Theseus and Ariadne, Minos and Phaedre, and Daedalus who was supposed to have designed the Labyrinth to hold the Minotaur. She had looked forward to this for a long time: to see the place behind the legends. Now all she wanted was to be in the throne room and see if their father was waiting there.

"I'd suggest," Grand said when Nikos had left to bring the desserts, "that after we've finished, we all get together for a game of hearts. Sam beat us rather badly last time and I, for one, intend to get even."

Jennifer smiled wickedly, "Going to neglect your knitting? I'm sure Maggie's really looking forward to wearing that sweater!"

"Yes," teased Maggie. "I was thinking of wearing it for my high school graduation!"

Grand looked ruefully at her hands. "I'm afraid I've had to abandon my knitting career for now. I only brought one package of band-aids!"

Maggie was feeling she could very well have cut out the dessert part of the meal by the time they'd finished and arrived at the game room. She was stuffed. Jennifer threw herself down on a chair and groaned. They moved the card table over enough that Grand could watch down the hall, and cut to see who would deal.

"I think," said Grand. "That we'd better do some planning for tomorrow." She looked at Jennifer, shaking her head. "You know my dear, I'm still not sure that I saw what I saw last night. Except that I have to believe my eyes and all the things you have told me. Anyway it's always amazed me that modern people can accept the concept of science fiction...you know...for instance the Star Trek idea of dematerializing someone...the 'Beam-me-up-Scottie' sort of thing, and yet ridicule things magical."

"I know Grand," smiled Jennifer, "that's why I've forgiven Sam and Maggie for hanging onto me...."

"That's a relief Jennifer." Sam gave her a cross-eyed look. "A real comfort...I'll tell my bruises."

Jennifer made a face at him and Maggie put in, "you are the only adult I know of, Grand, that we could tell."

"Yes," Jennifer said to Sam. "Grand still believes in Never-Never land..." she waved her arm, "...second star to the right and straight on 'til morning!"

"You're a terrible tease, Jennifer," Grand laughed. "But I confess to always wanting to be invisible. When I was a youngster there was a comic strip called *Invisible Scarlet O'Neil*, and she could press a nerve in her left wrist and become invisible. It's a wonder I don't still have marks on my left wrist, I spent so much time trying to find that nerve!"

Jennifer gave her grandmother an appraising look, "hmmm...it's a shame I didn't bring the spell...who knows? It might have worked for you!"

Grand shook her head. "I think we've got our hands full as it is. You explained some of the business of what happens, but tell me something. What if you had something with you, like Sam's key the other day, for instance, and you set it down or handed it to someone else? What happens then?"

Maggie looked at Jennifer. All three of them stared at each other. Finally Jennifer answered, "I don't think it's ever happened Grand. I'll have to try it next time."

"I think," said Grand, "that we might do that little experiment tonight before we go to bed. We can do it quiet-ly. You'll tell me a lie and go invisible while holding something...one of Maggie's books, for example...and then set it down. We won't have to say anything at all."

"And then I can tickle her feet!" added Maggie.

"If it works..." said Sam, his face lighting with enthusiasm, "...then it will be a perfect way to transfer the passport to...to your dad...when you find him."

Grand nodded.

Maggie couldn't stop smiling. It could work. It would be fine. If only. She caught Jennifer's look, they were thinking alike again.

Grand was explaining carefully. "It seems to me that there must have been a reason for the ticket to have ended up with you girls. A meeting with one or both of you would be less noticeable. Besides, Ghislaine's comments about the others looking for him, make me think we're being watched by more than Dr. Rossi. We don't know who the man was in the hotel in Athens, or who he was working with." She looked dubiously at Maggie. "I wouldn't even dare suggest this but we'll be close behind you. After the tour group has seen the throne room, Maggie, you sneak back and wait to see if...."

"...if Dad comes..." Maggie was delighted.

Grand nodded. "It would be very risky you being alone...."

"But I'll be there...invisible..." put in Jennifer eagerly.

"And if he's there, Jen can slip him the passport," added Sam.

Again Grand nodded. "Sam and I will stay behind with the tour, except perhaps you could dawdle a bit and slip back and check on them, Sam. Keep an eye on Brady and I'll keep Dr. Rossi occupied. If he seems to notice anything, I'll say the girls have gone looking for a washroom or something."

Maggie felt positively joyful. She could hardly wait to go back to the cabin and check things out. Suddenly she sensed a change in Grand. Someone was obviously coming down the hall.

"Do hurry up, Jennifer Dear," she said clearly, "it's your turn."

Jennifer nodded and quickly laid down a card. "You're doomed!" she growled at Sam.

Grandmother nodded toward the man who stood in the doorway. Maggie recognized Brady. She stopped in the midst of setting down her card. They all stared at him.

"Oh dear!" Grand said, smiling at him in a friendly way, "I do hope we won't disturb you. Sometimes, I'm afraid, our games get quite noisy."

Brady smiled and began to back out of the room. Maggie was sure he'd intended to come in but Grand had managed, very nicely, to make it look as if he was disturbing *them*.

"No," he said, smiling awkwardly, "I was just checking for someone..." he continued to back out, "Have a pleasant evening."

They watched him leave and began to play self-consciously.

"Oh! You rat!" Jennifer made a swipe at Sam as he laid down the Queen of Spades. That got things back to normal.

They knew that Brady was out of sight when Grand finally said, "The good news is he's well out of earshot, so we're free to talk, and the bad news is that after tonight I don't think we will be safe to speak freely in here."

"Sorry, Jennifer!" Sam said, giving her his best fiendish smile.

"Quite alright," she said with a haughty look. Then in her smarmiest voice, "I forgive you Sam."

"I think," said Grand, yawning, "that we'll just finish this hand. Tomorrow's going to be a very busy day. What are the scores Maggie?"

Maggie checked the paper and pretended to cry. "It looks like Sam's winning again."

Jennifer groaned.

"Don't take it so hard, Jen. I'm sure you'll..." he stopped and stared at Jennifer. "Oh, oh, you're feeling sick, aren't you?"

Jennifer nodded. "Here I go, again. Well, I guess we can do that experiment here as well as in the cabin." She held up her hands, waiting.

"So," said Grand, "I get to see the other part of it, do I? At least there's some warning. But how..." she looked puzzled.

Maggie wondered too, but Sam just grinned and said, "I'm obviously not forgiven for dumping the Queen on her!"

"Look, Maw, no hands!" Jennifer said, waving her wrists at them. Soon the arms had faded.

"I don't really believe this," said Grand, "but I must say I admire your nonchalance. You handle it very well, all of you!"

Maggie laughed. "You should have seen us the first time, Grand. Trying to figure out how on earth we would get her back before Mum found out! That's it, Jen, you're gone. Give me something."

"Okay, okay, let's see," came Jennifer's voice. "Of course!"

Suddenly, the sparkling vest landed on the table in front of Maggie.

Maggie reached out and picked it up. And then Jennifer's invisible arms were hugging her and they were doing their victory dance. "It works! It will work! Oh Jen!"

Jennifer was pushing her into a chair now and Maggie felt a foot poking in her face. "Hurry up!" she said, "I can hardly wait for tomorrow!"

Jennifer slept more soundly than she would have believed possible. She had expected a fitful night, full of dreams haunted by interrupted meetings with strangers who turned out to be her father, and fathers who turned into strangers as she approached. Instead she woke up refreshed even before Grand's little travel alarm clock sounded. She felt good; nervous but full of hope.

Part of the good feeling came from the fact that it was a relief to have Grand in on the invisibility thing. Not that she'd been carrying it alone. Maggie, and particularly Sam, had always been there for her – but now there was a purpose and a plan and it gave her a feeling of specialness that she'd only felt a few times in her life before. The day on the swing, for example. It was a feeling like that. Wonderful. And this time she didn't need the picture with her father to remind her. This time she would be doing something really important.

She looked over at Maggie. It always surprised her that anyone could sleep so – there was only one word for it – neatly. No wonder Maggie always had her bed made in no time in the morning. She didn't muss it. She hardly moved at all and when she turned over, she did it neatly, without disrupting anything, and ended up with the covers folded and smooth, her chin resting on her hand. She doesn't even muss her hair, Jennifer thought with disgust. By rights she should be the worst sister in the world, being so perfect and all, but she could be fun and even come up with the odd surprise. Like trying out the spell, for instance. Still, Jennifer had to admit that Maggie's most useful trait was her dependability. At least as far as Jennifer was concerned. The world would be a tough place without her.

In spite of the fact that she was awake waiting for it, Jennifer was the only one of the three of them who jumped when the alarm went off. Maggie groaned and pulled the covers over her head in a Jennifer-like way. Grand sat up immediately, turned off the alarm and smiled at Jennifer.

"My goodness, it's the first time I've wakened to see you look so raring to go, Jennifer," she said. "Did you sleep well?"

Jennifer was already out of bed. "I did," she said, rummaging in her drawer for a shirt, "splendidly." She began to hum merrily.

Grand laughed. "You remind me of a little verse my grandmother used to recite: "I wake in the morning early, and always the very first thing, I poke out my head and I sit up in bed and I sing, and I sing, and I sing!"

Jennifer made a face, "That's pretty bad, Grand! I call it smarmy!"

"We used to call it 'twee,' a good word, I think." She shook her head. "The worst of it is, that's how I feel most mornings...it drives people crazy, I find."

By now Maggie had given up and was out of bed too. Jennifer was pulling on her gypsy skirt. It could get awfully crowded in the cabin with three people moving around trying to dress, but Grand had disappeared into the bathroom.

"What are you going to wear, Maggie?" Jennifer asked. Meanwhile she was pointing to her own skirt and miming that Maggie should wear hers too. They'd be expert charade players by the time the trip was over, she thought. The tough part was to keep a normal-sounding conversation going at the same time.

"Oh, I think I'll wear my skirt," Maggie was taking blouses out of the closet one by one as Jennifer shook her head to reject them all, finally nodding at a plain white top. Maggie nodded in understanding as Jennifer waved the one she was planning to wear.

"Ask Grand if you can borrow that nice straw bag she got in Athens." Jennifer had picked it up and was demonstrating putting her floppy straw hat inside. Maggie looked puzzled, so Jennifer tried again.

"Oooh," Maggie said as the light dawned on her, "it does go nicely with my skirt...better than with yours...and lots of room in case I buy anything."

Jennifer nodded vigorously. She picked up her own purse, removed the passports Grand had passed to her last night, and tested to see if they could be trusted in the deep pockets of her skirt.

"There are always souvenir stands where we get off the bus, at least there have been other times." Jennifer looked ruefully at the few bills and coins she had left before she shoved them in her other pocket. Perhaps she shouldn't have spent nearly all her money on the vest. But when she looked at it she decided that she didn't regret spending all that money. She'd only have bought a bunch of souvenirs that didn't mean anything. Now she had something to keep that would always remind her of this trip. She picked the vest up and laid it carefully on the desk by the door. She'd put it on as soon as she'd finished brushing her teeth and getting ready. Of course, she thought, she wouldn't need the vest to remind her of the trip. She would never forget it. Especially if today turned out the way she believed it would.

They lined up and each took their allotted number off the pegboard. That way the crew could tell at a glance if the people who left were back on board at the end of the day, and how many more to expect. You had to show your token to the crew as you returned.

This was a part of the trip that Jennifer didn't particularly like. You lined up to get off the ship, you lined up to get on the buses. And then you lined up when you got off the buses to go into the museum or whatever. Boring. She didn't mind doing this sort of thing when it was field trips at school, but she didn't like feeling like a school kid now. Not today. Not the day that might be the very best of her life so far. Look on the bright side, Jennifer, she told herself, at least in Crete they were docking and didn't have to clamber in and out of the little launches that sometimes took them ashore. It would save time.

She followed Grand onto the bus. Maggie and Sam were close behind. Dr. Rossi had got on ahead of them and when she looked back she could see Brady not too far behind Sam.

When they arrived they were divided into tour groups. Maggie and Sam actually seemed interested in what the guide had to say about the clever Minoans and their system of plumbing, but Jennifer fidgeted. She was impressed by the size of the place and the thought that so many people had lived in the palace thousands of years ago, but right now she couldn't care less. She barely glanced at the beautiful dolphin paintings in the Queen's chambers, or the huge bull mural at the central court. All she wanted to do was get to the throne room.

Even then she had to wait until the tour group had gone through it before she went up to Grand to whisper that she was going to have to go back to the restroom they'd passed on the way in. It was a very long way and she wondered what would happen if she really had to go back. They were standing in front of a bathtub right now and the tour guide was explaining about the system of plumbing that the Minoans had used. Behind her as she slipped back through the crowd, she could hear a loud American complaining to his wife, "You dragged me all this way to look at some old bathtub!"

Maggie followed her. As they ducked through the doorway up the steps Jennifer noted that Sam had managed to stay very close to Brady. Grand and Dr. Rossi were standing close to the tour guide. It was good because she was starting to feel sick. Very sick. She quickly pulled off her hat and vest and watched Maggie put them in Grand's bag. By the time she'd finished her hands and feet were gone and she was feeling better. There was no one around. The tours were always spaced a distance apart to allow for stragglers. Now if they could just get to the throne room before anyone came.

"You're gone," said Maggie softly and they moved quickly back. The room was gloomy, especially after their brief time outside, and at first Jennifer's heart sank. There was nobody there.

"Oooh," it was more of a gasp than a word and Maggie stopped suddenly, her hand to her mouth.

Then Jennifer saw him too. He was standing back in the shadows, his back to them. His clothes looked as if they'd been slept in and his dark hair looked greasy and tousled.

Maggie began to walk faster, almost at a run. For a moment Jennifer's eyes filled with tears because she'd waited so long for this and Maggie would be the only one who could get to hug him. She reached into her pocket and felt the passports. They'd agreed that, to let Jennifer have some share in the moment, she would keep the passports until the last minute and then slip them into his hand, making it look as if it was Maggie doing it. It had to happen quickly, before anyone came. Brady, the next tour group – anybody. Jennifer darted forward around Maggie.

He heard them coming and turned. Maggie was almost there but Jennifer saw his face first.

"No!" It was a cry, a moan, and it held so much despair Jennifer didn't even recognize it as coming from her own throat. She threw herself back to try to stop Maggie.

Too late. By the time Maggie saw the twisted angry face of this man who was not their father he had grabbed her, clapped a dirty hand over her mouth and held her arms pinned vise-like.

Jennifer fought back the impulse to jump at him and just scratch and kick. He'd probably only hurt Maggie. Maggie was kicking and struggling as best she could.

"Stop!" the man growled. "Good girl, come quiet..."

Jennifer backed off, looking desperately for a weapon of some kind. She'd noticed some pieces of rubble outside the door but he was facing that way, he'd see it come floating towards him and Maggie would be in the way. Distraction. Maggie couldn't scream but she still could.

She took a deep breath and gave something between a Tarzan yell and a howl and darted for the door without waiting to see the reaction.

She was outside before she almost collided with someone and her heart leapt with relief. At first she didn't recognize him without the moustache but there was no mistaking the lightning-shaped scar by his mouth. It was the man from the hotel in Athens and he was rushing in speaking gruffly to the other man. She couldn't understand the language, but it was about Maggie, she was sure of that.

When he spoke to Maggie it was in English, harsh and with an accent Jennifer didn't recognize. "Co-operate," he said. "You want to see your father don't you? I'm sure he will wish to see you."

So that was it. They would use Maggie to make her father come to them and then... Jennifer had to take a chance with a piece of rubble, even if they saw it. She picked up a flat sort of stone, probably once part of a stone tablet. It was light enough that if they saw her and she had to she could throw it like a discus, but she hoped she'd get close enough to hold it.

The man from the hotel was holding a hypodermic syringe and bringing it toward Maggie, who'd started to struggle again. Jennifer moved as fast as she could.

Maggie's captor saw the stone as she came closer and his eyes widened, but the sounds that came out weren't any language at all. At least Jennifer hoped not. What he was seeing she knew was exactly what Sam had seen in the hall that day, except instead of a looseleaf binder coming down on somebody's head it was a stone. It was too heavy to get up as high as she'd have liked but it hit the back of the man's head hard enough to knock him down and send the syringe flying out of his hand.

The other man gasped in horror and backed away but he didn't let go of Maggie.

Jennifer stepped over to where the stone tablet had fallen when she'd swung it. The man she'd hit was lying quite still, unconscious, she hoped.

But now she needed another distraction if she was going to be able to pick up the piece of stone and use it again. And a scream wouldn't do this time. She needed to make him turn around and if she screamed he would face toward the sound. She needed something to throw to make a noise behind him. Her hand groped in her pocket and felt the little bit of money. The coins would work if she could throw them hard enough so that they would hit the wall behind him. She pulled her hand out and gave it her best underhand throw. And watched in horror as the bills floated down in front of his face. He did too, staring towards her but as the coins began to land behind him he spun around just the way she'd hoped he would.

Jennifer lifted the tablet again.

'm going to wish that I could take this tour again, Sam thought. It was hopeless trying to concentrate on what the tour guide was telling them, even though he knew that any other time he would have found it very interesting. Now he just wanted to get out of there and see what was going on with the girls back in the throne room.

"And now we will move on up these stairs to see the famous storage area of amphorae," the tour guide was saying. "Because of the destruction of the palace by fire after the volcanic eruptions in 1450 BC..." People were following her out now.

Sam could see Grandma say something to Dr. Rossi. She glanced back, caught Sam's eye, nodded, and then continued speaking to the Professor.

Sam began to back away through the crowd. It was hard because they were now moving forward. He didn't want to alert Brady by turning around, even though that would be easier. He'd just wait until Brady was ahead of him and then he'd turn. Except he should have seen Brady by now, they'd been standing fairly close together. Sam turned and scanned the people moving towards him. No Brady. Somehow, he'd managed to slip away without Sam noticing. He began to run, weaving through the crowded room. He had to get to the throne room and warn the girls and he had to do it before Brady got there.

At least, Sam thought with relief, I know where they are, Brady will have to look in several places and might not go straight there.

He caught up to Brady just as he was approaching the throne room, and slipped by him so that he got to the door first. What he saw stopped him in his tracks.

There was a man. Was it James Arnold? From what Sam could see he was hugging Maggie, but he was turned away from the door so Sam could only see her brightly coloured skirt on the other side of him. But that wasn't what brought him to a standstill. A good-sized piece of flat stone was being lifted and brought down on the back of the man's head.

Jennifer, he realized. But Jennifer would not be conking her father over the head. As the man collapsed, Maggie struggled away from him and Sam's inertia left him and he started into the room. Maggie met him halfway. She was half-sobbing and shaking hard and she clung to him, which, he decided, wasn't a bad thing at all.

"It's okay...it's okay," he said to her, "Jen got him."

He was aware that Brady had come in and had gone over to the man who'd just fallen. That was when Sam realized there was a second man lying nearby.

Brady knelt beside the man his hands moving quickly, searching him. He looked up toward Maggie, "are you alright, Miss?"

Maggie pulled away from Sam and looked at Brady suspiciously. He'd just removed a gun and a few other items from the man's pockets and slipped them into his own.

"I'm fine," she seemed calmer but Sam could tell she was measuring the distance between them and the door in case they had to leave quickly.

Brady moved over to search the other man. Suddenly, he stood and glanced around the room. "Where's your sister?" He seemed very alarmed. "They didn't get her?" He looked as if he was ready to run to the rescue.

Maggie shook her head. "No...no...she got away...she's gone back to Grand...to our grandmother." She was obviously much calmer. "There were only two of them," she added.

Sam noticed the hypodermic needle lying near the other man. So did Brady and he went over and bent to examine it. That was lucky, Sam thought, because something strange was going on.

Out of the corner of his eye he'd seen movement. The large straw purse Maggie'd been carrying had moved. Just a flutter. He stared. There were some coins lying about and as he watched one at a time they were moving an inch above the ground, drifting towards the purse.

"I'll get your purse for you, Maggie," he said quickly. He scooped it up and began to pick up the remaining coins. He felt himself being patted on the back and a couple more coins slid by him into the purse.

Brady was speaking to Maggie again. "If there were only two men, who knocked them out? There must have been someone else here."

Sam was glad Brady's attention was focused on Maggie

as a few bills were now coming toward him. Fluttering as if being blown, although, he thought, they were more likely being kicked along. Either way it would appear suspicious since there couldn't possibly be a breeze in here. He quickly went over and shoved them into the purse.

"Somebody else?" Maggie repeated.

Sam realized he'd better get back to her and give her time to stall that question.

"Here's your purse," he said quickly, going over and handing it to her.

"Thank you, Sam." She smiled at him as she took it. "Yes," she said turning back to Brady and speaking slowly, "...yes...I suppose there *had* to be someone else." She looked over at the man Sam had seen holding onto her when he first arrived, and shuddered, rubbing her arms hard as if trying to erase the memory of his grasp. She shook her head slowly trying to remember. "I...I didn't see anyone," she said slowly.

"No, perhaps not...but it means there's someone else in the vicinity...." He was looking at Maggie speculatively.

Did he suspect Maggie of lying, Sam wondered? Actually she'd been telling the truth. She couldn't have seen Jennifer at all.

"I'm worried about your sister," Brady really did look concerned. Was it about, Sam wondered, whether she was alright, or because he thought she'd found their father and gone with him? "Maybe I'd better take you back to your grandmother and make sure she's alright. The other person might still be around."

Maggie's protest came almost too quickly, "Oh no! Mr. B –" Her hand shot to her mouth and Sam's heart sank.

She'd almost said his name and there was no way that they could know his name. He hoped Brady hadn't registered the "B..." part.

"It's okay," Sam put in quickly, "I'll take her back."

Brady was looking at Maggie in a curious way but he nodded to Sam in agreement.

"Just as well, I'd better stay here until these two come to." He seemed to realize that some explanation was needed because he added rather lamely, Sam thought, "I'm a policeman and I've been after them...I expect you just stumbled onto them when they were exchanging drugs." He pointed to the syringe on the ground.

Sam put his arm around Maggie and moved her toward the door. He dropped it as soon as they were outside. No point in pressing his luck. She wasn't trembling anymore, though she did look back.

They both wondered where Jennifer was but they didn't have to wait long. She pushed in between them. "Keep walking," she hissed. "Are you okay, Muggins?" her voice was the most serious and concerned Sam had ever heard it.

"Yes, I'm fine, Thanks to you." Maggie smiled.

"Fine enough to put part two of the plan into effect?"

"Of course!"

"Then start now. I'm going back there to see if I can find out any more from Brady when those guys come to." Jennifer's voice was already moving away from them. "And Maggie," she came closer again, "I don't think you should say anything to Grand about this...I hate not to...but..."

"We'd all be on a plane back to Canada tomorrow...." Maggie said sadly. She nodded toward the throne room. "Are you okay going back in there?"

Jennifer was obviously already on her way. Her voice came back, "Why not? They can't see me and I'm not likely to laugh. I'll catch up later."

"Part two of the plan," Sam said looking around.

The next tour group had just come into view. Luckily there were a few places to go to before they hit the throne room.

"Come on," said Sam, "we'll just head around the corner on the stairs. That's where our group was going when I came back to find you."

In a moment they were around the corner. Sam stood watch and Maggie worked quickly. It didn't take long. She deliberately hadn't worn a hat this morning. Unlike yesterday she was the only one who had to switch identities, so it was only a matter of slipping into the vest and Jennifer's floppy hat. It was useful, Maggie thought, that most people identify you by your clothes. Jennifer had insisted that they made sure that everyone had seen them walking around together. Identical sandals, white tops and skirts that only showed their difference if seen side by side. Like twins, Maggie thought. Seen separately with hats covering their hair, only people who were very familiar with them could tell which one they were seeing.

It was a good thing it didn't take long because Professor

Rossi and Grand were coming down the stairs towards them. Obviously, Maggie thought, Grand couldn't stall him any longer.

"Oh Jennifer," Grand said as they came up, "there you are! I was beginning to get worried. Dr. Rossi was kind enough to accompany me." She looked puzzled, "but where's Maggie?"

Sam answered quickly. "Didn't you see her? She went on ahead, she must have missed you in the crowd."

Maggie flashed him a thank-you look. She was quite sure she could have fooled Dr. Rossi, because her voice was the same as Jennifer's – but their manner of speaking was very different. Maggie could imitate Jennifer's staccato style but it was nice not to have to do it too much.

"We'll run ahead and find her," Sam was already starting up the steps.

Maggie turned and ran after him. "See you soon, Grand!" she called.

She could hear Grand saying something to Dr. Rossi about "all these stairs." Good, she thought. She's stalling to give me a little time.

She turned the corner at the top, handed Sam the bag and hat and quickly slipped out of the vest and was around the corner again, waving. "Hi Grand, there you are!" Maggie waited until Dr. Rossi looked up and her grandmother waved back, then came back to where Sam was standing and slipped into the vest and hat again.

"That should do it," she said. "When they come back, we'll say Maggie had to go find a washroom. I think I should be Jennifer for a while since Rossi and Brady think she's the suspicious one."

"That could be a problem," Sam said, pointing to the handbag. "You've now established that Jennifer's carrying it. What are you going to do with it when you're Maggie?"

Maggie looked at him and started to laugh.

"Don't even think about it!" he protested. "I am *not* going to be seen carrying a purse! That would look even more suspicious."

Maggie had to admit he had a point. "Technically you're right," she said, "but we'll just have to hope that nobody notices, or just thinks we're taking turns carrying it. After all, Maggie had it before. Oh," she said, "here comes Grand."

"And no Dr. Rossi."

Grand came over and gave Maggie a hug. It felt good and it reminded Maggie that not long ago she'd feared for her life. The impact of remembering almost made her cry. It took her a minute to be able to catch what Grand was saying.

"...not there?" she said, her voice very soft and sad.

Maggie just shook her head, she didn't trust herself to speak.

"And Jennifer? Where is she now?" Grand looked worried.

"She..." Maggie thought quickly, this was going to be tricky. "She waited...Brady was going to talk to some men...and she...she decided to eavesdrop."

There, that ought to do it. Not that she'd turn invisible if she told an outright lie, but she didn't want to lie to Grand; although she knew that the whole truth would definitely be more than Grand would be able to accept right now.

The truth was, now that it was over and she was standing here in the sunshine safe with Sam and her grandmother,

Maggie almost felt that the scene in the darkened room, herself captive, seemed like some nightmare she'd just wakened from – like moving from unreality to reality. Except, she shuddered involuntarily and rubbed her arms, she could still feel that hand clamped on her mouth, and the relentless way that horrible man had held her. Get a grip, Maggie, she thought. She hoped Grand hadn't noticed.

Luckily Sam was distracting her. "Where's Dr. Rossi," he asked, glancing nervously behind her.

Grand looked back too. "He said something about going back to get a picture of the bull mural in the main court, now that the crowd had moved on. I suppose he's checking on Brady, though I must say I've never seen the two of them together."

Maggie looked at Sam. The next tour would be along in no time. She wondered how Brady would explain it if the men hadn't regained consciousness or if he was still standing around pointing a gun at them.

"Hadn't we better catch up with the tour?" asked Sam.

"I suppose we must," Grand said reluctantly. "Jennifer will catch up. You'll have to slip in the washroom and make her laugh before we get back on the bus. You've done a very good job of being two people, but that would be beyond even your talent, Maggie Love." She glanced back and sighed. "It would have been wonderful if he'd been there." She said softly. "I know you and Jennifer were really hoping he'd sent the ticket as a clue.

"Very appropriate, you know," Grand continued with a sad smile. "The word clue comes from clew which was the ball of twine that King Minos's daughter Ariadne gave Theseus when he was sent into the Labyrinth to fight the

Minotaur. She kept one end, so that if he was lucky enough to survive, he would be able to find his way back out of the maze. And so the word became clue – something that leads to the solution to a puzzle." Again the sad smile. "Your dad would have loved the connection."

Maggie nodded. "He liked puzzles and riddles and word games, especially, didn't he?" She said remembering. It made her feel sad too. Even sadder because she was sure now that the ticket hadn't been sent by her father. It was a trap to catch her or Jennifer, and that, in turn, would have been a trap to catch their father.

Grand had nodded. Maggie knew she was having trouble speaking because when she did, her voice cracked a little.

"I'm glad Jennifer waited, just in case," she said, "but I hope she doesn't wait too long. We've got to be on that bus in twenty minutes.

They had caught up with the tour by now. People were straggling back up the hill. Some like Sam were standing staring around. Maggie looked too. The palace was on a rise of ground and yet it seemed to be in a bowl with the forested hills rising around it. She wished she could see it as it had looked all those years ago. The palace, beautiful with its hundreds of rooms, so vast that in later years people would look on its ruins and see a labyrinth. Just as they looked on the frescos of young people leaping and somersaulting over the horns of bulls like gymnasts or dancers, and made up a story of a creature, half-bull, half-man who lived there. She couldn't help believing it was a beautiful place, even though she would remember it instead as the place where the dream of finding her father had turned into a nightmare. She felt a hand on her arm pulling her along and thought it was Sam reminding her to leave. She turned to smile at him, letting him know that she was alright and instead found herself left behind facing nothing.

"Come on!" Jennifer hissed in her ear.

Nearly everyone had disappeared, gone on to board the bus. There were still one or two people left in the washroom. They crowded into a cubicle. Not an ideal situation to try to make someone laugh, Maggie thought.

She grabbed Jennifer's foot, but it was hard to keep her touch light enough to tickle. She found her hands were shaking. She heard the last of the group leaving.

"Maggie! Jennifer!"

It was Grand's voice and Maggie knew the worried tone wasn't just acting. Obviously she'd stalled the bus driver as much as she could.

"We're here, Grand!" She answered. She was about to add that she couldn't get Jen to laugh when she finally got the tickling right and Jennifer began to laugh and struggle. In fact she kicked against Maggie so hard that the door came open and she staggered backward out against Grand.

"Ooof!" She let Grand prop her up a moment and then shoved the bag through the door to Jennifer. "There you are! We'd better go stall the bus driver, Grand."

Her grandmother hesitated. "Will you be alright Jennifer?" she asked. "Is the pins and needles feeling starting yet?"

"Yes," came Jennifer's voice. "Go ahead, I'll be there in a minute."

Grand was busy explaining to the driver, so Maggie had to walk down the aisle to their seat alone. Judging by the looks Maggie got, people were not pleased at being kept waiting. She tried to smile pleasantly. She hated it when people were upset with her.

She nodded at Sam across the aisle and took her seat, sliding across to the window. Good. She could see Jennifer coming out of the washroom. She had her hat pulled down over her face. Good idea Jen, Maggie thought. Nobody would notice the fact that she probably didn't have a face yet. By the time she got on the bus and started down the aisle she did. Maggie watched her sister coming towards her. She hoped nobody else noticed that the vest was on a bit crooked. Even for Jennifer she looked – Maggie decided that best word for it was "scattered."

Maggie stood up. She'd give Jennifer the window seat without even arguing about whose turn it was. It gave her a chance to look around the bus.

"Have I got something to tell you!" Jennifer mumbled as she slid by.

Maggie took her time about sitting down. She'd managed to turn completely around in the process of letting Jennifer in. There was Dr. Rossi, sitting a couple of rows back, staring at her. But the seat near the back that Brady had occupied on the way there was empty and a quick look told her that he was not anywhere on the bus.

When Jennifer had gone back to the throne room one of the men was coming to. Doing it very well too. No groaning or movement, just lying very still gathering his wits, waiting. She only knew he was awake because she'd gone very close and noticed his eyelids flutter and heard the change in his breathing.

It was the man who'd held Maggie; the man who'd been prepared to kill her, to use her to kill their father. Jennifer stood quietly, looking down at him. This is what it feels like to hate someone, she thought. It's awful. She understood now why people said that hatred did the most harm to the person doing the hating. It was like the feeling you had when you had hurt yourself and the pain spread through your body until you couldn't think of anything else. But this was heavier, like a great stone growing inside you. Hard and cold; icy cold. At the same time, she thought, it's fierce. She knew if he moved again, if Brady somehow lost control, she would have no trouble hitting that man again and this time she wouldn't have the excuse of protecting Maggie. She would hit him because she wanted to hurt him. The realization shocked her.

It wasn't just hate, it was anger. Fury because for one wonderful moment when she and Maggie first saw him standing in the shadows, she'd thought they'd found their father.

Anger and hate: fire and ice. Nobody could live with the feeling, Jennifer decided. She pushed it away. Think about Dad. He wasn't coming here. In all probability he hadn't sent the entry ticket – that had been a trick. But she couldn't let that matter. What mattered was that he would try to find them. He loved them. She thought of the watch: he had loved them since the moment they were born.

There, that was better, the anger and hate were leaving.

"Put your hands on your head and sit up," Brady was saying, "and do it very slowly."

Jennifer felt a surge of relief. The man was smart enough to wake up slowly but not smart enough to fool Brady. Good. But he lay still and didn't obey. Instead he mumbled something in a language Jennifer couldn't understand. What language did they speak in Syria, she wondered? Arabic? Anyway, maybe he came from somewhere else.

She felt a surge of disappointment when Brady spoke again. He was speaking whatever language it was, probably just repeating his command this time. But this meant she wouldn't be able to understand the questioning she was sure was going to take place. How was she ever going to find out anything?

The man obeyed, sitting up hands on head. Now the other man, the man from the hotel in Athens, groaned loudly. Either he was not as clever as the other, Jennifer thought, or he was trying to provide a distraction.

Brady spoke rapidly and he obediently sat up like the other. Jennifer moved over toward the door, ready to dart out in an instant. She'd realized with a jolt of fear that she might be invisible but she wasn't bulletproof and she shouldn't take chances. Knowing no one could see her had made her careless.

Someone was coming; she could hear footsteps just outside. She peeked out. If it was her father she was prepared to make a dash to warn him. And she still had the passports in her pocket. For a brief moment all the hope was back. Not long. It was Dr. Rossi who loomed in front of her. She stepped back.

Evidently, he'd been close enough to hear Brady's last question, because he spoke quickly, adding something. Again it was incomprehensible to Jennifer. She began to wonder if there was any point in being here at all.

"Any idea who they are?" Rossi asked.

Brady shook his head. "One Syrian passport, one Iranian...doesn't mean a thing...probably each got half a dozen more."

"What happened?" Dr. Rossi had moved over beside Brady.

"Our friends," Brady said, nodding towards the two men, "were stone cold when I got here. Obviously had tried to kidnap one of Arnold's kids...the quiet one...the other one wasn't here...I figure she maybe went with Arnold...or...."

"No," Dr. Rossi interrupted him, "I saw her just a minute ago. She's with the grandmother and the Elwin boy."

Good for Maggie, Jennifer thought. The plan is working.

"What!" Brady's voice registered surprise but his eyes and gun didn't stray from the men on the floor. "Are you sure? I don't know how she got out of here. Last I saw them the two girls were together...I got here just behind the boy and there was only the one girl and these two were out cold." He shook his head slowly. "It had to be somebody...the kid couldn't have done it and the boy didn't have time. The grandmother?...no she wouldn't have left the girl with them...."

"Impossible, she was with me the entire time." Rossi shook his head. "I think we'd better check with CSIS again over her. She's very sharp. And taking the kids on this trip would be the ideal cover. Still, I can't imagine her risking them, if she was involved."

Dr. Rossi glanced towards the door. For a moment Jennifer feared that he'd heard her make a sound. "We'd better get these two out, there's a tour group on its way."

Rossi was holding a gun now. Jennifer wasn't sure if it was his own or if Brady had slipped it to him. He spoke rapidly to the two men. Obviously he was telling them to get up, one at a time, at least that was what they did. Then Brady stepped in close behind one and Rossi the other. As they met the tour group outside, they began speaking again, as if in normal conversation. Again Jennifer couldn't understand a word.

She had trouble getting out. She'd waited too long and the people were filing in close together. She actually bumped someone, who then apologized to the person next to them and got a strange look. When she finally caught up to the four men, they were headed for a black van that was parked in the lot closest to the buses. She didn't recognize the man who opened the back doors for them until he turned. Stavros.

In no time, the two men were handcuffed and in the back of the van and Stavros was climbing into the driver's seat.

Rossi glanced at the tour bus and then back to Brady. "I don't for a moment believe that they didn't see who hit them. One of them must have seen something. See what you can find out. I'll see you back on the ship." He shook hands with Brady and turned and walked casually toward the bus.

People were getting on board now, some already in their seats looking out the windows. The little scene between Brady, Rossi, and the other men would have seemed perfectly relaxed and normal, Jennifer realized. Nobody could have seen the handcuff part.

Jennifer searched the bus windows to see if Grand had boarded yet, then headed down the path again. She hadn't seen them when she'd followed the men. The route Rossi and Brady took to the parking lot hadn't been the main one. Good, there they were. She felt a surge of relief as she saw Grand and Sam coming toward her.

"We'd better get back and seem to be waiting for the girls at the bus," Grand was saying, "Maggie can wait a bit longer." She looked worried. "I hope Jennifer's alright."

Jennifer resisted the impulse to try to reassure Grand. The sooner she got Maggie into the washroom the better.

Maggie was standing staring into space, but when Jennifer grabbed her she seemed to come out of her trance.

It was times like this, Jennifer decided as they crowded into the cubicle in the washroom, that she wouldn't have minded being Grand's Invisible Scarlet O'Neil. There had to be an easier way to reverse the spell. Maggie was jabbing at her foot in a way that would probably leave scars. Jennifer restrained herself from kicking back as hard as she could. Maggie hadn't exactly had the best day of her life, no wonder she was a bit violent. Still, being understanding wasn't going to help make her visible again. If only there was some way to calm Maggie down a little. Then she heard Grand's voice and somehow Maggie slowed. Maybe she was a bit more relaxed herself. Whatever it was, the tickling worked at last. She gave an involuntary kick and began to giggle.

Jennifer got on the bus a few minutes later. Walking down the aisle felt good. It was great to be back, she decided, as she slid by Maggie. Invisibility had its disadvantages. You were on the outside of things, but you didn't want to be on the outside of the important people in your life. She looked around her. Sam and Grand and Maggie were like a circle taking her in. She could sense their eagerness to find out what she had learned. She glanced behind her. Dr. Rossi was looking at them. Jennifer gave him a dazzling smile. Might as well keep him guessing.

She couldn't wait to get a chance to talk. Bad news that they'd had to abandon the game room, but it would probably be bugged by now. Maybe they'd get a chance to talk wandering around the deck. She settled down to wait impatiently. She'd better make use of the window since Maggie'd been generous enough to give it to her. The scenery didn't interest her as much as the black van she caught a glimpse of as it turned off the road ahead. Jennifer peered after it. It was heading up a long tree-lined drive to a very fancy house at the top of the hill. It must have a lovely view, she thought, but there were no houses nearby. A very solitary spot.

They met at Maggie's deck spot as soon as they could. Jennifer still didn't know what Maggie had told Grand about the encounter in the throne room, but obviously nothing about the kidnapping attempt. She was sure Grand would have been much more upset if she knew about that.

She decided only to talk about the most recent bit and let Grand assume Maggie and Sam had told everything there was. Still, she had to tell Grand that Brady had captured those two men. Even if she didn't go into details, Grand needed to be warned that the Syrian connection had appeared. After all, a mother would be almost as good a hostage as a daughter to bargain with.

"I wish I knew why they are so sure that your father is even in the vicinity," Grand said when Jennifer finished. "I doubt that they'd be here if they didn't have *some* information."

"Oh! I just remembered something." Jennifer looked at her grandmother. "What's CSIS?"

Grand looked at her strangely. "Canadian Security In..." Grand stopped. "...something or other, I believe. Why do you ask?"

"Dr. Rossi wanted Brady to check about you." Jennifer laughed, "Maybe he thinks you belong!"

"Wonderful!" Maggie joined in with a giggle. "Our Secret Agent Grandmother."

Grand gave her a funny smile. "Thank you so much...SAG for short...how appropriate! Let's see now...perhaps I should bring out my knitting as a cover-up!"

Jennifer lay back on the deck chair and laughed. It was wonderful to feel it rising up inside her – first as a chuckle, then louder and louder until she was rolling about. She knew it was mostly relief from all the tension of the day but she didn't care. It felt so good. When she could finally speak she said, "Not a chance, Grand, that's probably what made them suspicious to begin with!"

Grand reached over and hugged them both. "Never mind casting aspersions on my handicraft skills. I want you to listen to Sam's plan for Istanbul."

"It's your plan too," said Sam quickly and began to explain.

I t was nice of Grandmother Arnold to give him credit for the plan, Sam thought. If she hadn't mentioned that she was concerned that the passport might not be enough to get the girls' father out of Turkey, he'd never have dreamed it up.

"Your grandmother thought it would be much easier to get your dad away if we'd met him here in Greece, than if we met him in the two Turkish places we're going...."

"Istanbul and Kusadasi," added Maggie.

"...Yes," Sam continued. "So I started thinking. Passengers on the ship just walk ashore and get back on."

"But the tags?" put in Jennifer.

"I've been watching. They check them *coming back* but you take your own and nobody noticed yesterday when I took mine and another. I put it back right away and pretended I'd made a mistake in case somebody was looking, but," finished Sam triumphantly, "I could have kept it and somebody else could have handed it in."

Jennifer looked doubtful. "Fine," she said, "so he's on board. Somebody's bound to notice – and anyway where's he going to sleep?"

Sam was ready for that one and feeling pretty confident. Grand had been sceptical at first too. "A lifeboat. There's one on the foreward port side of the sundeck I managed to get into. It's got a cabin that's big enough for a person to hide in fairly comfortably. We could smuggle him blankets, food, and water...."

Maggie shook her head. "But what if the person whose tag he's taken complains?"

"It would have to be somebody we've found out isn't going ashore...like Dr. Rossi on Mykonos," Sam explained.

"Right, Maggie," nodded Grand. "I know it's tricky, but it's certainly better than leaving him to try and get out of Turkey. Even with the passport stamped for recent entry, they may check and find they have no record and then..." She shuddered involuntarily.

Sam hoped the girls hadn't noticed and went on. "I've been watching that lifeboat from time to time and nobody seems to go near it. I don't think the crew have looked at it since we had our lifeboat drill the first day."

"I'm still cheesed off about that!" grumbled Jennifer. "Making us run around getting into our lifejackets and standing at the lifeboat stations when I wanted to be standing at the rail watching the ship leaving the harbour. My first major voyage by ship." She paused dramatically and put her hand to her brow. "Another potential highlight of my life wasted!"

Sam ignored her. He was used to Jennifer's "wasted life" scenes. In his opinion Jennifer's was one life that was lived to the utmost and *any* potentially dramatic moment was seized on and shaken like a dog shakes a rat.

"It could work." He'd been saving this bit for the last. "I noticed that there's a passenger who's been skipping the shore trips. I think he's sick or just doesn't like all the walking, and," this was his best piece of detective work and he'd been saving it for the last, "his number token hangs right below mine!"

Even Jennifer looked impressed.

Grand looked at her watch. "Oh my goodness! We've haven't changed for dinner and our seating is due to begin any minute." She hurried them along, glancing around her. "I think it's safe to talk as we walk if we keep a sharp watch, so I'll tell you what I think each of you should do when we get to Istanbul."

Sam's assignment was the taking of the token, of course. Then he was to keep a close eye on Dr. Rossi and try to keep him out of the way if the girls or Grand managed to make contact with James Arnold. Other than that, he was just to mill about and help Maggie pretend to be two people when the time came.

"And Jennifer Dear," continued Grand. "I think it would be best if you didn't start the invisibility thing until we actually see your father...coming to me to tell your lie will create a diversion...." She looked concerned. "You will be able to manage that, I suppose?"

Jennifer nodded. "Sure Grand. Telling you even a tiny lie makes me feel as bad as a whopper with Maggie or anybody else."

Grand gave her a smile. "Thank you Dear, that makes me feel better...I think!"

Sam had to leave them then to head down to his and Dr. Rossi's cabin, so he didn't hear what Maggie's assignment was, although he had a pretty good idea what it was going to be.

He unlocked the cabin door and went in. No sign of Dr. Rossi, but of course he'd already be at dinner. Sam went to pull a clean shirt off the hanger and threw it on the bed. That was when he noticed it. Dr. Rossi had left the little drawer ajar. Sam wouldn't have noticed because his drawer had been the same but when he reached in to pull out his notebook he'd closed it tightly and so now the other showed. Dr. Rossi probably thought he'd closed it because it had been even with Sam's.

Sam checked the bathroom, made sure the room door was locked and carefully wrapped a Kleenex around his fingers before he tried to slide it open. It slid smoothly and quietly. And the contents were different than Jennifer described them. The only things in the drawer now were two guns. He supposed those were the ones Brady'd taken from the two kidnappers.

He shut the drawer quickly leaving it just the slight bit ajar that it had been before. But now it showed because his drawer was closed tight. He thought a bit and decided to pull his drawer out enough to match and then hurried out to meet the others in the dining room.

Sam woke up early. He wanted to be up on deck to take some pictures as the ship sailed into the harbour at Istanbul. The skyline was world famous. He'd been reading up and he was sure he would recognize Topkapi and the Blue Mosque and Santa Sophia, at least.

Since his luck with the Brady picture, he had decided to try to include other passengers in some of his shots. But today, he wanted to make the skyline pictures memorable – after all you could buy them anywhere – so he'd use Maggie and Jennifer in turn in the foreground. He was favouring

Maggie. Jennifer was wearing the sunflower hat and while she ignored Maggie's criticism about looking bedraggled, even Sam thought the hat had seen better days.

"Alright, one of you on each side of Santa Sophia as we go by," Sam ordered, looking into the viewfinder.

"It says here that it's Hagia Sophia," Maggie'd been buried in a guidebook since breakfast.

"That's because," said Sam waving at Jennifer to move in a bit, "hagia means saint...at least the study of saints is hagiology...or maybe that's a book about saints. Okay, ready, set...Cheese!"

"That's what I like about you Sam," said Jennifer, "you're a gold mine of useless information...confused at that!" She flashed her best movie star smile, peering out from beneath the sunflower.

Sam ignored her. He resisted pointing out that occasionally his useless information came in handy. Besides, the way he looked at it, even useless information was better than not knowing anything at all. And sometimes, like just now, it explained something. As a matter of fact, when he'd come across a hagiology book last summer at Grandad's in Wolfville, he'd got caught up by the lives and especially the gory deaths of some of the saints. He'd never dreamed that it would give him a chance to show off a little by being able to explain something to Maggie.

Nicking that extra token had been a cinch, he decided as he boarded the bus. He was a bit nervous that this would be the one day passenger #84 would decide to go ashore, but he told himself that if that happened, he'd just pretend he'd taken it himself by mistake, and let Mr. Arnold have his own number.

The bus took them first to the blue mosque of Sultan Ahmet. As far as Sam was concerned they spent much too much time there. There were, according to the tour brochure, four stops: the blue mosque, Hagia Sophia, the palace of the sultans which was called Topkapi, though he hadn't managed to find out why yet, and a shop selling Persian carpets. Unless they were the flying kind, Sam figured he would as soon give that a miss.

Now, after twenty minutes of listening to the tour guide's commentary on the mosque and the services there, he decided to move back in the crowd from the ship. He could see Grand and Maggie standing politely, listening. Jennifer was standing nearby bent over as if studying the mosaics on the floor. Sam lounged against a pillar and casually sidled around it to see what he could see. He was surprised to see Brady moving forward from behind the string of people. He hadn't seen him on the bus, or last night at dinner. Was he just now coming back to join the tour? Sam wondered how he'd got here from Crete. But he supposed there were ferries, and there was an airport, so he could have flown.

He wanted to get up ahead to warn Jennifer, but at last the tour guide was finished and everyone was turning to leave. He'd be a fish swimming upstream and there wasn't much point. If he just stayed by the pillar she'd have to go by.

Except he must have missed her somehow, next thing he knew he was at the tail end of the line with Maggie and Grandmother Arnold just a little way ahead. He decided to stick as close as he could to Brady. If he hadn't done that, he would never have noticed him drop a folder of matches.

"You've dropped something," Sam said politely. He tried to get to it first but Dr. Rossi was somehow there and picked it up.

"This yours?" he went after Brady, who acted properly surprised and thankful when Rossi handed it back.

Or had he? Sam really couldn't see if anything had changed hands. Brady put something in his pocket but maybe it was just his empty hand. Sam had to keep moving so he slipped ahead.

Outside the sunshine dazzled and there were dozens of hawkers waving postcards, tour books, scarves and souvenirs in their faces. People who stopped to buy were mobbed even worse than those who pushed through. He could see that Grand had already run the gauntlet and was standing by the bus door. Jennifer's sunflower bobbed on ahead of her already on the bus.

Maggie was having trouble getting through. There was an especially persistent man with a straggly beard poking some ugly scarves in her face. She wouldn't even look at him and Sam ducked between them and pushed her ahead to the bus.

Sam took his seat with relief. Next stop Santa Sophia. He noticed Dr. Rossi boarding and quickly turned to ask if he could borrow Maggie's guidebook. He was afraid if he looked in Rossi's face the man would read the suspicion there.

It was not until the bus pulled away that Sam realized Brady was not on board.

Maggie had seen Sam slip the extra number token off the board that morning. She was standing right behind him and if she hadn't been watching very closely, she wouldn't have noticed. She was a bit concerned when she realized that things were going to be different going ashore here. After all it was another country. Their other shore trips had just been part of Greece. Her heart sank when she realized that they had to pass through a corridor with a wicket at the other end.

"You'll have to show your passports," said Grand, digging in her purse. She was carrying the girls' and Sam's with hers. They'd decided that was easier.

There was an officer from the ship and a Turkish official, but it was obviously just a formality. Maggie held up her passport showing the photo page, the officer said "Canadian" and that was all. They did not even take it from her for closer examination. She hoped it would be the same procedure when they came back on board.

She always enjoyed the bus trips and it was her turn to get the window seat. Wonderful interesting streets and shops, street vendors selling little green plums, sweets, and all sorts of other strange things. It took quite a while to get to the square in front of the Blue Mosque.

The square was jammed with vendors and now they weren't so picturesque. They were insistent and pushy. Maggie had seen a scarf she thought she might like to get for Mum, but when she reached for her purse to see what she had in Euros (the guide had told her they'd be accepted), they moved in and she felt so crushed she couldn't breathe. The price he'd quoted had been way too high. She was supposed to say one half that and then he'd lower his, and so on, until one or the other gave in and agreed. Maggie hated haggling. Why couldn't they decide on a price and you paid that or else you decided you couldn't afford it and it was over?

She could see the tour guide standing on the steps ahead waiting for everyone to get together, but she couldn't move. She was beginning to panic when she felt Grand's arm around her shoulders.

"Come on Maggie Dear," she said, "this is not the best place to shop anyway."

Inside the Mosque it was better. She listened intently to the story of its construction, admired the fine mosaics and the soaring domes. The story of why there were six minarets was fascinating. She liked that sort of thing. According to the tour guide, Sultan Ahmet had ordered seven minarets, the architect felt that would spoil the look and pretended he had heard the word "blue," and so the beautiful Blue Mosque was built with only six minarets.

Out of the corner of her eye she could see Jennifer moving restlessly about. They'd worn the same outfits as yesterday but with different tops and Jennifer had put on that disgusting old hat that she'd had for years.

"You're *not* going to wear *that,*" Maggie had protested. "It doesn't match *anything!*" She'd have added that she thought she ought to have some say into what Jennifer put on her head since she'd be the one that ended up wearing it half the time, but they were still in the cabin.

"I love this hat!" Jennifer said vehemently. "It's special!"

Maggie had given up. There was no talking to Jen when she got that stubborn. After thirteen years Maggie had figured out when to back off.

She glanced around but Sam was out of sight somewhere in the crowd behind them. Part of their instructions from Grand had been to separate and change arrangements as much as possible. They were still not sure how Dr. Rossi figured in this whole affair. There hadn't been time for Jennifer to do her invisible thing last night and listen to what he told that bartender. And Brady had not showed up. Something was strange. The only thing that was clear, Maggie thought, was that they wanted to get to her father. It seemed to her that if Brady and Rossi's intentions were good, they'd have come out and talked to Grand about it. And Grand seemed to feel that Rossi and the others should be kept at bay. That was enough for Maggie. Still, she could stay by Grand for a little while. The guide was explaining where people went to pray, the women separate from the men.

Outside it was awful again. She'd have liked to stop and look around. Sam was taking pictures. She was slowed down by the persistence of the street vendors, but she found if she kept her eyes straight ahead and kept walking she could make some progress. She wished the buses hadn't had to park so far away. She could see Grand waiting up ahead.

"No!" she said angrily as one man rushed up to her, almost blocking her path. He actually put out his hand to grab her, and she remembered the awful feeling yesterday and the awful grip that had held her. "No," she shook her head, almost sobbing. And then Sam was beside her, helping her along, pushing her through towards the bus.

She took her seat and sat trembling as the bus pulled away. How silly, she thought, that was nothing like yesterday. Nobody would try anything in that mob, in broad daylight. She'd been perfectly safe. But she couldn't shake the feeling that there'd been something wrong. Something that didn't fit.

By the time they arrived at Santa Sophia she felt calmer. Partly, she supposed because this was the oldest and most interesting of the places they would be visiting in Istanbul. Once a famous Byzantine church, then a mosque, and now preserved especially as an historic site for both, like a museum.

"Look at that!" said Sam. He was pointing above them as they went in. A beautiful golden mosaic gleamed like new above the archway. The tour guide was explaining that now that it was no longer a mosque, some of the early Christian mosaics that had spent centuries hidden by plaster had been uncovered.

"It's beautiful!" she breathed. "It looks almost like new."

Sam was busy trying to get a photograph and she moved on ahead with the group.

Really, she thought, as she looked at the magnificent green malachite pillar that had been brought from the

Temple of Diana at Ephesus fifteen centuries ago, this was a very special place. Hadn't the Temple of Diana been one of the Seven Wonders of the Ancient World? Only the pyramids were left, but here at least was a piece of one of the Wonders.

Maggie sighed happily. Here it was cool and dark, but so huge that somehow it didn't feel as crowded as the Mosque had, and there had been hardly any people selling things outside. Once you paid to get inside the gates it was safe. Not that there weren't other people, even some poorly dressed ones who were obviously not tourists. But it was special, she felt very calm and happy.

She reached out to place her hand on the pillar. I'm touching centuries of time, she thought. And then, staring at her hand, tanned and brown from the sun, she realized what had been so wrong in the square in front of the Mosque. All the peddlars were dark, and their hands tanned even darker than her own. The man who had reached for her had a white hand, unnaturally pale, although it was smeared with dirt. Someone who'd been a prisoner would have hands like that. The dirt was probably just part of his disguise.

"Jennifer!" She cried out involuntarily. She had to find Jennifer. And Grand. They had to go back. Hot tears stung her eyes and she hated herself. She hadn't even looked at him. All she had noticed was his wrist, pale and thin – so very, very thin.

She felt her arm being grabbed and turned, half-fearful, half-hoping. Nobody there. Jennifer's voice hissed in her ear.

"Quick, open the handbag and pretend you're looking in it."

Maggie did and felt something pushing by her as the vest appeared in the bottom. She opened it wider. Jennifer was making it shake suspiciously. There. The awful hat was there.

"Lean against the pillar as if you were feeling sick or something, while I talk to you," whispered Jennifer urgently.

Maggie did it. The pillar felt smooth and wonderfully cool, but all thoughts of past centuries were forgotten. "You weren't supposed to go invisible until we found him..." she tried to speak without moving her lips. She hoped anyone seeing her would just think she was trying to keep from throwing up.

Jennifer's voice was so excited you could tell it was a struggle for her to keep to a whisper, "I did! He's here! He found me!" Maggie could tell it was taking every bit of willpower Jen could muster to slow herself down. She squeezed her eyes tight shut and tried to keep her face from changing expression. What she really wanted to do was grab her sister and do a Victory dance to end all Victory dances, but she knew it wasn't time for that. Not yet.

"I gave him the passports and the money and the note telling him about coming on the ship," whispered Jennifer, "but you've got to get that token from Sam. I can't do it, it'll show."

Maggie waited a minute then straightened and looked around. Dr. Rossi was standing halfway between Grand and her looking at her. Sam was further off busily taking pictures from every imaginable angle. She took a deep breath and set out.

"Isn't this wonderful, Dr. Rossi?" she gushed as she passed him. "All this *history!*"

He looked at her strangely and then smiled and nodded.

I hope I didn't overdo it, she thought. Grand was waiting for her when she arrived. "What's wrong dear? Aren't you feeling well?"

Maggie nodded and a look of understanding passed between them. Grand strolled casually over to stand not far from Dr. Rossi and Maggie headed over to the nearest doorway into the long, colonnaded hallway. There were a few people moving up and down but she was able to press behind one of the doorposts and slip into the vest and hat. She ducked back into the main part of the building and moved carefully behind the pillars. Grand was talking to Dr. Rossi and had moved so that he had to face away from the doorway.

Sam looked up from his camera. "Hi Mag...Jennifer." His voice took on a tone of excitement. "So it's happened?"

She nodded. "But we need to give him the token now, just in case we can't connect again at the ship."

"Of course," Sam reached in his pocket. "Here," he said, softly, holding out his camera, "you can take my picture, I'll drop it in your hand when you take the camera."

Maggie took it and felt the token fall into her palm. Sam moved off to stand between two pillars and she clicked the shutter.

"Try to get one at an angle so you get the light streaming in that window," he said loudly.

"I can't seem to figure out how to..." she began.

Sam came over and took the camera. "Don't sweat it," he grinned, "I've used up all the memory anyway!" He handed it to her and backed away saying loudly, "back up and see if you can get a couple of distance shots."

Obediently, Maggie backed up.

"More," called Sam.

There was a very effective echo. She was sure Dr. Rossi could hear. She backed up. She was in a dark corner now.

The guide had explained that this was the place the women of the harem used to sit. Beautifully screened with lattice work – she hoped Sam had managed to get some real pictures of this.

"Jennifer!" The voice was soft and very close and it was one she hadn't heard for a very long time, but she would have known it anywhere. She turned joyfully to face him. Would she even have recognized him if she'd looked in his face at the Mosque? He had a dark scruffy beard, but there was no hiding the familiar blue eyes or the love in them as he looked down at her.

"Maggie?" There was surprise and she took a moment to give him a hug. She didn't want it to end but she knew it had to. She handed him the token without a word and he pushed her back out.

Sam was standing where she'd left him, adopting various poses. Anyone would have assumed the photographer was just out of sight.

She came up to him holding out the camera.

"Good?" he asked.

"Good," she said smiling at him.

Jennifer knew the old hat looked awful. It had been floppy to begin with but it was totally limp and shapeless now. And the sunflower had a cheerless unsunflower-like droop to it. On top of it all it didn't fit her properly anymore, but then she'd had it since she was nine years old. She loved it. And she was determined to wear it today despite Maggie's protests. She knew when to back off with Maggie, but today she'd just ignore her sister.

Somehow, as she pulled it on she felt stronger. She'd felt that way the day her father bought it for her. They'd been on their way to a movie, just the two of them. Maggie and Mum had chosen to go shopping for the afternoon. It had started to rain. She could remember the fresh smell and the drops sliding down her face. And they'd puddle-jumped the way they used to do when she was little. She'd seen the hat in a store window then and somehow the sunflower had seemed just what was needed on a happy rainy day. She hadn't had to beg for it. He'd looked and smiled and followed her into the store.

"That hat is *you* Modom!" he'd said, imitating a smarmy saleslady, when she'd tried it on. "It's very you," he said giving her a hug and pulling out his wallet.

Maggie had come home with a new hat that day too – a plastic rain hat – very practical.

The hat had been too large for her then, but her hair had frizzed up in the rain. Thank goodness, Jennifer thought now, tugging at it, I wouldn't be able to get it on anymore at all.

She couldn't explain all this to Maggie and she definitely couldn't tell her why she believed that somehow the hat would bring her father to her today.

It had to be today. There would be other people looking for them soon. She'd strolled through the lounge last night hoping that she might see Stavros and Dr. Rossi. If they'd been there she'd have persuaded Grand to let her eavesdrop. She wanted to know what they were going to do about the two men who'd tried to kidnap Maggie. But Stavros wasn't tending bar. Someone else noticed it too.

"The other bartender? I hope he isn't ill?" a woman asked. Jennifer recognized her as the woman with the harsh voice who'd been there the other day, trying to strike up a conversation with Dr. Rossi.

"He had to stay on Crete," was the reply from the new bartender. "I believe there was a death in his family."

The woman murmured something about being sorry and went back to her table. Jennifer kept going. That was a relief. She hoped that Stavros and Brady would keep those men away. And with any luck the people who'd sent them wouldn't have found out they were missing. Today, all they had to worry about was keeping Dr. Rossi occupied. And finding Dad.

She thought the bus ride to the Blue Mosque took forever. She'd been right behind the tour guide as they crossed to the Mosque. She wanted to get inside, it seemed to her that would be the most likely place.

The tour guide's voice droned on and Jennifer crouched down as if to examine mosaics. She couldn't understand how Grand and Maggie could even *pretend* they were enjoying the commentary. From this position she could keep an eye on people by their feet. Dr. Rossi was dressed quite casually today but his beige canvas shoes had a distinctive tassel tie. She saw something fall nearby and she saw Sam go forward to try to pick it up. Too late. Whatever it was, Rossi picked it up and seemed to hand it back. Not really. From this angle she could see he still had it in his other hand.

She stood up, staggered a little from having been crouched down for so long, and tried to catch up. She had-n't seen the man who'd dropped whatever it was, but she'd seen the shoes. Dirty white runners. Unfortunately, half the people on the ship wore some kind of runners, they'd been told to wear comfortable walking shoes. She ducked past Dr. Rossi to try to catch up to the shoes, but by the time they were outside she knew it was hopeless. She gave up and headed for the tour bus. She was the first one on board.

Everyone was making a fuss over the mosaics as they moved down the hall at Santa Sophia, but Jennifer barely glanced at them. She couldn't wait to get inside. As soon as the tour guide was busy pointing at something, she edged by. She decided to find herself a spot and watch shoes as people came in. The best thing to do was to sit at the foot of one of the pillars and pretend to be fixing her sandal. Too bad it was one of the Greek toe-and-strap kind with no buckle to fiddle with.

"Are you having a problem?" Dr. Rossi was standing not far away staring at her.

His voice startled her. "No," she said quickly rubbing her foot. "Something sharp must have got under my toe."

There'd been no sign of the runners anyway, so she got up and decided to play a little duck-behind-the-pillars-and-bug-the-spy with him. It worked. She almost laughed, he was just too obvious and looked ridiculous standing there watching a bored teenager killing time. Soon he moved on and began to watch Sam's picture-taking efforts.

Jennifer got on the end of the line of a group of people who were taking turns at what the guide called the "wishing hole." She hadn't heard the beginning, but apparently if you put your thumb in the hole partway up one of the pillars, you would get your wish. Trouble was you had to turn it completely around, and people were going into some fairly complicated acrobatics just trying.

"Dad, please." She murmured inaudibly as she put her thumb in and turned completely around. There was nobody else so she did it again.

She was about to do it a third time for luck when she realized there was another person behind her in line. Then a voice said very softly, "That hat is *you* Modom!"

Jennifer couldn't move. It was as if she'd turned to stone, her thumb locked inside the wishing hole, joined forever to the pillar.

It seemed to hold her and then she only breathed it. "Dad!"

It was all she could do now to stay still. She had waited so long for this. It wasn't fair that she couldn't let her joy show. But she knew there might be someone watching, so she finished her turn, caught a glimpse of his face, thinner and bearded but so dear she almost couldn't look away. She was facing the pillar again and she quickly slipped the envelope out of her pocket and held it in front of her. He understood and took it as he moved into place and put the thumb of his other hand in the hole.

"Don't leave – there's something else," she murmured. "Find me later."

She moved away, wanting to laugh and cry and scream at once because it was happy and desperate and awful all at the same time – because he was here but he wasn't safe, not yet. Not for a long time yet.

Sam had actually got Dr. Rossi to turn and stare at the dome overhead, pointing at something with his back to Jennifer. Good move, Sam, she thought with relief. But Grand was too close to him. Still, why would Rossi find it strange that she let her grandmother know she was going to the restroom she'd seen just inside the front gate?

Then she pretended to leave, and found a quiet spot to wait for the lie to work. Maggie could do the rest. Jennifer wished she'd thought to get the token from Sam. Now they had to risk making contact again. But she'd be invisible, she could set things up and watch to see that no one interfered.

Maggie was still gazing at the pillars when Jennifer emerged, invisible at last.

She wished she could approach her father, but it would only startle him, and he might give himself away. So she had to stand by as Maggie took advantage of the shadows to hug him. Then she'd pushed Maggie back out before Rossi got suspicious.

She checked him, just to be sure but he was still standing talking to Grand. Maggie had stashed the hat and vest and emerged from behind yet another pillar as herself.

"Maggie Dear," Grand said, "you'd better tell Sam and Jennifer to come along, we should be getting back to board the bus." She began to move toward the archway with Dr. Rossi.

Jennifer stuck as close as she could. She'd just remembered that Dr. Rossi was carrying a gun. Besides she wanted him safe outside so that her father could leave. The note had told him to take a taxi and meet them back in the dock area and that would be tricky. The sooner he was safely on board the better.

Everyone was passing through the gate to the buses nearby. Dr. Rossi seemed to be sticking to Grand like glue. Sam was taking one last picture.

Maggie was wearing the hat again. She paused at the door of the washroom and called to Grand, "Go ahead, Grand, Maggie and I will be right with you."

A few minutes later she came out. Jennifer followed close behind. Good. Grand had persuaded Dr. Rossi to go ahead of her on the bus and was just starting up the steps. They were going to be the last ones on, the driver was obviously holding the doors. Grand spoke quickly to him, stepped back off, and Sam made it out just as the doors were closing.

Jennifer could see Dr. Rossi go back to his seat, pause, and begin to move forward, but it was too late. He couldn't do anything without making a fuss – he was stuck on the bus to Topkapi.

Grand turned as if going back to the washroom to look for her missing granddaughter. "It worked," she said, "I told him Maggie was sick and I was taking all of you back to the ship." She walked toward a row of taxis. "I wonder...?" she began.

Jennifer was so close to Maggie she risked speaking. People would think it was Maggie. "Gone." she said quickly. She had seen her father getting into a cab as they came out.

They climbed into the cab. It was crowded with all four of them in the back seat even though it looked like only three. Jennifer plopped herself down on Grand's lap, which caused an involuntary, "Ooof!" on Grand's part.

For one awful moment Jennifer thought she was going to laugh. That would have been bad. There would have been one spooked Turkish cab driver, for one thing. For another, she had to stay invisible. It was her job to keep an eye on her dad and make sure he got safely on board the ship.

"I'm afraid," said Grand, "that Dr. Rossi will probably skip the Topkapi tour. The minute that bus arrives he'll be in a cab on his way to the ship. It doesn't give us much time."

The driver must have been taking a roundabout route, Jennifer decided. It was taking much longer to find their way than even the tour bus had taken from the dock. Grand was starting to look concerned. She tried to lean forward to talk to the driver and Jennifer slipped over onto Maggie to be out of her way.

"You did understand me?" Grand said carefully. "I said the dock...eesKEHleh ...ships...gehMEE!"

The driver said something in Turkish and just kept going. The streets were narrower and meaner now. Finally he stopped beside a small gate.

"You get out now," he said clearly.

Jennifer's heart sank. This was even worse than on Crete. They were completely away from anybody who might help them. Nobody moved. Then the driver got out of the car, opened the door on Sam's side and yanked him out.

Jennifer quickly slipped over the back into the front seat so as to be out of the way.

"So," said Grand haughtily, her voice completely in control as she climbed out of the cab and confronted the driver, "you do speak English! Well, let me inform you, young man, that this will cause international repercussions and..."

Good for Grand, thought Jennifer admiringly, she's bluffing just like a good card player. Not all bluff either. She's got an ace up her sleeve – an invisible granddaughter.

Jennifer grabbed the keys out of the ignition as she slid out the driver's door. He was facing Grand, trying to push her aside to get Maggie out of the car, and Jennifer threw the bundle of keys as hard as she could against the ironwork gate. It made a wonderful loud clanging noise that caused the driver to spin around. Now, if only I had something to hit him with. She grabbed a flashlight from beside the front seat and turned but the driver was already on the ground groaning and holding his neck. Grand was standing rubbing the side of her hand and looking pained.

"Do you want me to knock him out?" asked Jennifer waving the flashlight.

The driver was staring bug-eyed at the flashlight jerking around above him.

"Oh Dear," Grand sounded distressed for the first time, "I suppose we must." The driver responded by cowering even more abjectly on the ground.

"Why don't we just lock him in the trunk?" Maggie suggested. "It won't look good to just leave him lying about on the street."

Sam had already picked up the keys and so it took him only a few seconds to open the trunk.

This will never work, thought Jennifer brandishing the flashlight. She hoped she could still stop him once he stood up.

"Get in the trunk!" commanded Maggie, "or I shall tell our Djinn to strike you down!"

Jennifer was so shocked she stopped waving the flashlight. Was Maggie out of her cotton-picking mind? She was glad to see Sam was holding a large rock. Oh well, might as well play along. She tried for the deepest, most resonating voice she could muster.

"Get...in...the...trunk!" she intoned. To her amazement, the driver crawled whimpering to the back of the car and proceeded to climb into the trunk. Sam slammed the lid and locked it and the four of them were in the car with Grand at the wheel.

So far, so good, Jennifer thought, trying to wiggle out from under Maggie who'd sat on her by mistake. She cringed as Grand ground the gears and backed the car around slamming it into the gate as she did so.

"I didn't know you knew karate, Grand," Maggie said politely as they careened down the street.

Grand sucked on the side of her hand. Jennifer wished she'd keep them both on the wheel. "I'm afraid I didn't finish...only took a class or two. Let that be a lesson to you...never be a drop-out!" She waited for their groans at that remark to subside. "I'm afraid though, my Dears, that we're in a good deal of trouble yet. I haven't the foggiest idea where we are. I assume that if I keep going in a downhill direction we'll hit the harbour some way, but I think we'll have to figure out something soon." They drove for some time with no sound except the screeching of wheels around corners and the grinding of gears. Grand was not the world's best driver, Jennifer decided. To her relief the streets were becoming more and more crowded and Grand had to slow down.

"Look for a landmark everybody," Maggie suggested.

"How about a minaret?" Sam asked.

There was a touch of bitterness in Grand's laugh at that. "There are hundreds of minarets in this city, I'm afraid."

"How about six minarets?" he said, pointing to the hill above them.

They didn't *park* the taxi at the square in front of the Blue Mosque, Maggie thought, so much as *abandon* it. Grand handed her the keys and hurried for a tour bus that was about to pull out. It was one of those from the ship. The groups had been divided up so that all would not arrive at the same place at the same time. This bus was obviously one that had the Blue Mosque as its last stop.

"Do you think we could get a ride back to the ship with you?" she could hear Grand's voice calling up to the driver. "We missed our bus...if you have room..."

Maggie could hear the driver put up an argument and Grand's "...grandchildren...just three of us."

"You'd better get rid of those keys," Jen's voice hissed in her ear.

Maggie didn't want to. What if the bus driver didn't let them on? At least if they still had the taxi, they could follow the tour bus back to the ship.

"Come on Maggie," Sam was waiting for her by the bus door. Grand had already climbed on.

She glanced around and there he was, watching her. Brady. She rushed up to him and thrust the keys at him. "There's something in the trunk of that taxi," she said pointing, "that might interest you...*Mr. Brady!*" She only gave herself a moment to enjoy the startled look on his face at the mention of his name, and then she was off, dodging through the peddlers and running past Sam onto the bus.

They'd been lucky to get on. There were only three seats left and they had to sit separately. She wondered for a minute where Jennifer was and then felt her sister plop down on her lap. The lady sitting beside her looked a bit shocked and Maggie smiled sheepishly at her, making a mental note to get even with Jennifer sometime. Pinching her hard was an immediate impulse but Jen would just pinch back. Maggie settled herself grimly for a very uncomfortable ride.

She felt Jennifer get off just before the bus pulled up beside the other returning tour buses at the wharf. Good, Maggie thought, she'll be at the front door when it opens, otherwise she'd be in trouble.

There were some taxis pulling up behind the buses. And she noticed with surprise that Dr. Rossi was getting out of the first one. Strange, she thought, he should have been here much sooner. Dad too, yet she recognized him emerging from the third or fourth one.

"Keep walking!" she mumbled to Sam who'd caught up to her. "He's here, but Rossi's right ahead of him...Jen will make sure he comes on board." The plan was for Sam to be waiting once Dad got on the ship, to lead him to the lifeboat. It was too bad they couldn't use Jennifer but she'd just have to follow along without letting him know she was there. Maggie felt sorry for her. Jen would want so much to be able to talk to Dad, but for now she'd have to resist.

Grand got off the bus just as Dr. Rossi came by.

"Ah, Mrs. Arnold," he said replacing his somewhat angry expression with a smile. "I trust your granddaughter is alright?"

Maggie had a momentary feeling of distress. Which one of them was it that was supposed to be sick, anyway? She'd forgotten whether she was supposed to be wearing the hat now or not.

"Ah..." he continued, looking at her. "There she is! Feeling better now, I hope? It's Maggie isn't it?" He stopped and looked around, "But where is your sister?"

Grand stopped too. Luckily people were still getting off the bus. "Oh dear! I'd better wait for her. Jennifer's always dawdling...just go on ahead."

Rossi obviously wasn't about to go. Maggie looked back. Her father was coming awfully close. She ran back and grabbed Grand's hand. "Oh come on, Grand, she'll catch up...she always does." She was sure that Rossi would be expecting Grand to make contact and wouldn't let her out of his sight even for a minute, and she had to get them out of there. She put her hand to her forehead, "I...I'm still not feeling very well..." she staggered a little, not too much, she hoped.

Grand caught on immediately. "Oh dear! Dr. Rossi, do you mind coming with us...in case...in case she faints...I'm sure I couldn't carry her...." she had her arm around Maggie making her stumble even more. "Sam, you'll wait for Jennifer, won't you?"

Dr. Rossi came reluctantly. He's suspicious but he can't very well refuse, thought Maggie. She realized that she didn't have to fake all that much either, she'd spent most of the time hatless because they'd wanted to make it easier for her to switch characters. And the sun was burning hot. But this would work out very well, she thought as she showed her passport. She'd let Grand take her back to the cabin to lie down, and then reappear as Jennifer making sure that Dr. Rossi saw her.

She tried not to think about what else might go wrong before they had Dad safely hidden on the ship.

Sam stood by the bus door pretending to wait for Jennifer to get off. Luckily the last of the passengers were still straggling down the steps as Maggie, Grand, and Dr. Rossi disappeared around the corner into the corridor to have their passports checked before boarding the ship.

He waited until Mr. Arnold was quite close before he turned to go. There'd been a brief glancing look but Sam could only hope that Jennifer's dad had recognized him. The worst bit was right ahead of them. If the people at the wicket checked the names on the passports against a passenger list there would be trouble. The best thing to do, he decided, would be to create a diversion. There was quite a lineup of passengers behind him now. He was pleased to see that both the officer from the ship and the Turkish official were different ones from when they had come ashore.

"Excuse me," he said politely, showing his passport, "did a lady and a girl come through here yet?" He didn't give them time to answer, he wanted to hold up the line so that they'd get behind and let people go through more quickly. "I was supposed to wait by the bus, but everyone seems to be gone and I must have missed them...I think the girl was sick...she almost fainted...did you see anybody like that...the tour was good but really long...she's probably just tired..." He was trying to think of more.

The plan was working, he could hear a lady in the line-up behind him say loudly to her husband, "Why are they holding up that boy? He's from the ship, I've seen him lots of times. Really, this is very inconvenient!"

"...and I'm worried...I don't see how I could have missed them...but I shouldn't go on board in case they come and wait for me...and can't go on board because I'm not there...and...."

The ship's officer finally managed to interrupt. "They've gone ahead young man, don't worry!" he said impatiently.

Sam hurried on, but turned just before boarding to look back. It would fit in with his concern about meeting some-one, if anyone noticed, and it gave him a chance to see that the plan had worked. Mr. Arnold and several others had moved quickly through. The line was stopped again as the loud lady asked questions about the Persian carpet she'd just bought.

He waited until he was directly ahead of Jen's dad and then moved on into the ship. Funny, he'd always imagined boarding ships would be walking up a gangplank with peo-ple watching below on the pier, but here you walked direct-ly on, onto carpets on one of the lower decks inside the ship.

He walked over to the board and slowly hung his token. That would give Jen's dad a chance to see what the numbers were, so that he could hang his without being conspicuous. A real passenger would know where the token went by this time.

He moved slowly out of the way, and used his ploy of looking back toward the people coming on board, to observe that the token was being placed beneath his own with no hesitation. He turned and went up to the next deck, then pressed the button for the elevator. If they could get on alone, he could talk to Jen's dad. The elevator was empty. Sam stumbled slightly getting on, something had bumped him. Of course – he'd forgotten Jennifer. He moved over to allow her into the corner and pressed the floor for the sundeck just as Mr. Arnold got on and the door closed.

"Hello Sam," he said softly. "It's good to see you."

They shook hands. It felt silly and inadequate for the way he felt just now, but it was all there was time for.

Sam quickly reached in his pocket and pulled out a couple of photos he'd printed off his camera. There wasn't much time, but he'd had the idea that Jen's dad should be alerted to Rossi and Brady.

Luckily nobody got on on the next floor. "We know they're agents," Sam said, "but we don't know who for – CIA maybe."

Mr. Arnold slipped the two snapshots into his pocket without looking at them as the door opened and they got out and went through the doors onto the deck.

Passengers were still coming on board below, so it was deserted. Sam led him to the lifeboat he'd chosen and watched as he slipped on board and disappeared into the little cabin. He knew there was water and some fruit, bread, and cheese. They hadn't been able to leave anything really perishable. They'd smuggled the stuff aboard by means of Jennifer, so nobody would notice. She'd even left a pillow, a blanket, and a couple of paperback books of Maggie's.

He stood for awhile staring at the skyline. He hoped no one ashore had noticed the activity at the lifeboat. But unless they were watching with binoculars it should be alright.

He felt Jennifer patting him on the back. "The pictures were a stroke of genius, Sam!" she said.

Yes, he'd rather thought that was a good idea, but it was a rare thing to get anything like praise from Jennifer. He felt pretty good. He looked up and down the deck before speaking. "So what do we do now?"

"Act normal, I guess. Why don't you go down to the cabin? I want to keep an eye on Dr. Rossi. Maggie's going to pretend to be sick and stay in the cabin, but really she'll put on my hat and wander around being me. I'll meet you at the deck chairs in an hour."

Sam nodded. Several passengers were coming out on the deck. He strolled around to the other side of the ship, entered and went down the stairs to his cabin.

The phone was ringing as he came in the door. It shocked him and it took a minute for him to realize what it was. Phone calls weren't exactly common on board ship. It was probably for Dr. Rossi and he wasn't sure if he should answer, but finally he picked it up.

The voice sounded a bit staticky but he recognized it right away. "Sam? May I speak to Sam Elwin, please?"

"Grandad?" This was wonderful. What a great surprise. "It's me! It's me, Grandad! Everything's okay, isn't it?"

"Just fine, my boy. Has everything been going well? I've phoned a couple of times today. I just got back to my computer from several days on the dig and found your e-mail and the pictures you sent. Very nice. Wonderful thing, electronic communication!"

Sam tried to remember what pictures he'd sent, mostly from when they'd first come on board the ship. The girls and Grand, one of his cabin. He'd caught one of Dr. Rossi out on the deck and included that too.

"But something's puzzling me Sam. I think you made a mistake labelling one of them. I showed it to my friend and he says that man isn't Tony Rossi at all – you must have mixed up the pictures."

Sam felt a chill go through him. "No. I didn't, I didn't," his voice was rising nervously. He had to get it under control. Grandad would wonder why he was so upset. He swallowed hard. "I labelled it right...it's him...are you sure...?"

He stopped, the words frozen in his throat. He could hear Dr. Rossi's key turning in the lock as the door handle moved and the cabin door opened.

Jennifer watched Sam leave. It was the hardest thing in the world to have been so close to Dad and not be able to talk to him, to touch him – she hadn't even hugged him yet. But he was safely on the ship. That was the main thing. Now all she had to do was make sure nobody checked the lifeboat until they got to Rhodes day after tomorrow. There he'd be able to catch a ferry to Athens and they'd meet him at the Canadian Embassy there. He couldn't stay on the ship until Athens because Grand said they really did check you and your luggage there when you disembarked.

She went over to the lifeboat. She could easily get aboard but she couldn't open the cabin door and he'd be hidden. She wanted to see how he was, if he was comfortable – just to look at him and see he was safe – but that would have to wait.

The new bartender who had replaced Stavros was on duty and Dr. Rossi was sitting in his usual place. Jennifer wondered why. Unless the new bartender was an agent too, it seemed a waste of time, but she supposed he had to continue the pattern so people wouldn't be suspicious. She was beginning to feel discouraged when the bartender came over and spoke to Rossi.

"Would you like another drink, sir?"

Jennifer moved closer, maybe this was it. Rossi just shook his head, signed the bill and left. Very disappointing, she thought. She was about to follow him when she saw Brady out on the deck coming towards the other door to the lounge. She waited. He came in and went directly over to a table in a quiet corner to sit down with a woman. Jennifer recognized her. It was the gabby lady who sometimes bothered Dr. Rossi. She decided she'd stay and listen. Dr. Rossi was probably just going back to his cabin anyway.

They didn't speak at first, just nodded to each other. The waiter came over to take Brady's order and then they sat quietly waiting for him to bring the beer.

Jennifer hadn't paid too much attention to the woman before. She was one of many middle-aged single women on the ship. Quite a few of them seemed to be eager to spend time with Dr. Rossi. She'd thought it was pretty funny, really. Some of them were alright looking, but this one was kind of plain, tall and definitely not thin. She was what Grand called "a big woman." Even her feet were big, Jennifer noticed. And then she was glad she was invisible because anybody would have noticed her staring. The woman was wearing a pair of dirty white runners and Jennifer had seen them before.

"Did he give you the message?" she asked without looking at Brady. She'd lit a cigarette and was blowing smoke at him.

"The one you tried to pass me at the mosque?"

"That was meant...for him to intercept it." She looked at him through narrowed eyes, blowing more smoke. "Now we see what he passes on to you. Everybody's being checked, you see." She paused and then said softly. "Stavros is dead."

Brady started to cough and slid his chair back out of the way of the smoke. He cursed under his breath. "What's going on? Did the men I caught get away?"

"It looks as if they were meant to. Somebody did a double-cross. And it had to be someone here. Somebody who figured Stavros could just disappear. But they didn't count on large Greek families. Stavros' uncles are raging. He was related to half of Crete, it seems. Now this goes beyond international intrigue..." She smiled and picked some tobacco off her lip, "...now it is a Greek blood feud!"

"Well, I've got some news too. Maybe I'll just keep it to myself for a bit. I'm still trying to figure out what goes with the Arnold gang. The quiet kid presented me with a terrified Turkish cabbie locked in his own trunk, who fed me the most ridiculous story..." He shook his head. "But I'm not even as interested in how the grandmother and the kids got him in the trunk. What I want to know is, who hired him to kidnap them in the first place?"

"Our double agent?" The woman had quit blowing smoke and just stared straight ahead.

Jennifer was grateful. Any more smoke and she'd be coughing herself. She didn't want to back away too much so she'd moved almost directly behind the woman. That way she could see Brady's face very well. She was sure that he'd been as shocked at the news about Stavros as she was. She had a sick feeling in her stomach. She'd almost come to trust Brady and Rossi, after all, they'd obviously been against the men who'd tried to kidnap Maggie. Now it seemed they had doubts about each other. It seemed you couldn't trust anybody.

"Another thing...the kid knew my name. How?"

The woman shrugged. "Probably checked the passenger list – after all you did rescue her."

Brady shook his head, "No...she already knew it then...today she used it deliberately."

"She could have been trying to delay you...from following them back to the ship."

Brady slapped some money on the table and stood up. "I'm going to stick to those girls like glue, just in case. Never mind Rossi."

The woman lit another cigarette. "Watch your back," she said softly.

Jennifer had twenty minutes left before she had to meet Sam and get visible before dinner. She had intended to just wander around the ship, and she did for a little while. She saw Maggie looking hot and tired in the sunflower hat beside Grand on the deck chair, and Brady had stationed himself on an upper deck where he could keep an eye on them. No sign of Sam yet.

Somehow her feet carried her to the sundeck. It had occurred to her that since her dad wouldn't look out, she could talk to him even if she was invisible. In fact, it was better, since no one could see her and she'd be careful that nobody was close enough to hear. The thought made her so happy she was almost running by the time she reached the lifeboat.

"Dad!" she said, "it's Jennifer!" She knocked the "shave and a haircut two bits" knock he'd taught her.

"Fine honey," his voice was muffled. He knocked back.

"There's nobody around, I can talk for a minute..." she said quickly. "Is there anything you need? Is everything okay?"

"Fine...fine...all the comforts of home."

Jennifer smiled. It was so good to hear his voice, to know that she was this close to him. Wonderful.

"But Jen...there's something...Sam gave me some pictures...said he thought the men were CIA. Maybe the one he marked 'Brady' is right, but the other... That man is definitely not Anthony Rossi, the archaeologist. I met him. He was imprisoned with Gerard and I in Syria. I don't know who this man pretending to be Rossi is, but he's not up to any good. I recognize him from Syria. too."

Jennifer couldn't speak. She heard footsteps approaching, for a moment she ducked automatically, forgetting she was invisible. Luckily Dad had heard it too, because he stopped and waited until she whispered, "go on," before he continued.

"I was flying some VIPs around, very top level, hush-hush...my co-pilot and I weren't even supposed to see them...but we did...one of them is the man pretending to be Rossi. I think that's why Gerard and I were thrown in jail. We wondered why the real Dr. Rossi ended up with us, but maybe it was just so someone could use his identity. If this guy you call Rossi was a mole in the CIA...that would explain it!"

"It also explains why he wants to get to you first!" Jennifer felt herself shivering in the warm sun. More people were coming along the deck. "Can't talk now. I'll come by later." Jennifer turned to go, then she stopped and whispered, "I love you." She wasn't even sure if he'd heard.

So Rossi was everything Brady suspected and more, and, the thought hit her like a thunderbolt, he was sharing a cabin with Sam. Sam! She started running. A few people turned and looked around them at the sound, but she didn't care. She took the stairs two at a time down to the deck below. There was Brady still keeping an eye on the deck below that. She almost bumped a lady as she ran past. It was lucky there was nobody on the next flight of stairs, she couldn't have stopped.

The hour was up and Sam should have been there with Grand and Maggie, but as Jennifer swung around the corner she saw that he wasn't.

They knew she was there before she said a word, she was puffing so hard. "Maggie!" she gasped, "get your book over as if you're showing Grand something...Brady's up above watching... get your heads together...and listen both of you!"

They didn't interrupt her. She told them everything Brady had said and then dropped the bombshell Dad had told her, about the man pretending to be Dr. Rossi. "And..." she finished, feeling sick, "Rossi went down to the cabin...and Sam wasn't on deck and he was supposed to be here!" She was having trouble keeping her voice from rising to a wail.

When she had finished, nobody moved for a moment. Then Grand stood up and faced the upper deck. Jen could see a movement as Brady stepped back.

"Mr. Brady!" her voice was loud and clear and not to be fooled with, "come down here, please. I believe it's time we had a little talk!"

Jennifer didn't believe it would work, but there he was coming down the stairs towards them.

Grand didn't mince words. As he approached she held out her hand for a formal handshake. "I am Lorraine Arnold," she said, "this is my granddaughter Maggie and this..." she caught herself in time, Jennifer couldn't be introduced, "...and you are CIA, I presume?"

Jennifer didn't wait. She decided she'd slip downstairs. She'd just remembered something. She still had a key to Sam's cabin, if she could just remember where she'd put it.

"Sam...? Sam...?" Sam could hear his Grandad's voice through the phone, but he couldn't speak. It was all happening too fast. He needed time to think and there wasn't any time. One thing he knew was that he didn't dare look up at Dr. Rossi as the man entered the cabin. His face would surely give him away. He turned to the phone and knocked his notebook off the bed so that he would be bent over for a moment or two.

"Sam...? Sam...? Grandad's voice was insistent.

"It's okay Grandad...." He spoke from the bent-over position so any strain Dr. Rossi heard in his voice would be blamed on that. "Just a minute, I've dropped..." He'd managed to nudge the notebook under the bed so now he was on his knees reaching for it. Good, Sam thought, his voice was almost normal, he turned towards Dr. Rossi but couldn't, from this position look right at him. "Oh hi, Dr. Rossi!" He hoped Grandad would catch on but he kept talking anyway. He didn't want any more questions about Rossi or the picture. "We've just come back from Istanbul...Santa...Hagia Sophia...was amazing!" He hoped the excited tone of voice he was trying for would cover his nervousness. He sat on the bed and flipped open his notebook. "You were telling me about some special things to look for at the ruins of Ephesus when we dock at Kusadasi."

Please Grandad, Sam thought to himself, don't pursue the Dr. Rossi stuff. Sam was lying on his bed now, leaning a bit away from Rossi's side of the room. He still hadn't dared look directly at the man. Who was he, anyway?

The pause on the other end of the phone was almost palpable. Sam knew Grandad was puzzled, more than that, probably; ill at ease over the mistaken identity. Sam prayed he wouldn't ask to speak to Dr. Rossi and demand to know what was going on. If that happened, Sam decided, he would say goodbye, hang up, and get out of the cabin as quickly as possible. He almost sighed with relief when Grandad spoke. He'd obviously decided to follow Sam's lead.

"I haven't been there for awhile, but the Austrian Archaeologists have done a splendid job. Be sure to get pictures of the Library of Celsus, it's magnificent and so is the amphitheatre. And," he added, "you might get a kick out of the old community toilet. Everyone sitting around visiting or chatting. You can still see the excellent drainage system where the streams beneath the seats provided the 'flushing.'" Grandad chuckled and Sam's heart sank. He hadn't wanted him to get too upset and ask too many questions about Dr. Rossi's identity right now, but it *was* serious and Grandad seemed to have forgotten it entirely.

Sam was scribbling "Library of Cel-something" and "amphitheatre" in his notebook, but he risked a glance up at Dr. Rossi. He did not like the way the man was staring at him. He didn't like it at all. He was glad he had the notebook. He wrote "community toilet" and took his time putting a series of question marks after it. He realized that he should be saying something in response to Grandad, who hadn't spoken for awhile. Maybe that's why Dr. Rossi was looking so suspiciously at him.

"Right Grandad!" He wished he could make his voice sound more normal. Even to himself he sounded like a bad actor in a play. "The Library of Celsus, amphitheatre..." he looked down at his notes and mumbled, hoping to cover his nervousness and not sound too phony.

"What's your next stop after that?" Grandad's voice was back to the concerned one he'd shown earlier.

That reminded Sam of something that had been bothering him. Kusadasi was still Turkey and it would be Thursday before they landed on Greek soil again. "Rhodes," he said, "day after tomorrow." He realized that Jennifer and Maggie's dad would still be in danger if he was discovered stowing away and put ashore in Turkey. Again, he tried to hide his face and pretend to be making notes. He didn't dare glance up at Rossi. Out of the corner of his eye he could tell that the man had not moved. Probably still staring down at him. Sam scribbled nervously – names of the islands they'd visited, places in Istanbul, anything just to keep writing and keep his head down.

Grandad was saying goodbye now. "...just wanted to check up on you......take care Sammy!" There was a click and the line went dead.

Sam managed only "Goodbye Grandad." He couldn't believe that Grandad had forgotten all about the Rossi mix-up, but it looked that way. Now what was he supposed to do? Time, he needed time. He clapped his hand over his mouth and rushed past Dr. Rossi for the bathroom. He locked the door and began to make retching noises so that Rossi really would think he was sick. Then he realized he'd better not make it too realistic, the way his stomach felt right now, it wouldn't take much to really throw up. He turned the taps on full blast and leaned his head against the cool metal of the shower stall.

Calm down, he thought, do some breathing exercises or something. He made himself relax. What could Rossi know from the phone call? Nothing. He knew something funny had gone on with the girls and the taxi. Yes, he'd be suspicious, but he couldn't have heard anything from the phone call. Grandad's voice was pretty loud, but after Dr. Rossi had come into the cabin he hadn't talked about Rossi or the fact that the picture showed the wrong man. Sam's warning had done the trick. He began to feel better. He would march straight out to the door of the cabin, mumble something about getting some fresh air up on the deck, and still be in time to meet Grandmother Arnold and the girls.

Having a plan helped. He flushed the toilet, turned off the taps, and opened the door.

The plan didn't work. The man pretending to be Dr. Rossi was leaning against the cabin door, arms folded, looking straight at him as he came out of the bathroom.

"I think it's time you answered some questions Sam," he said quietly. It was only when he moved that Sam realized he had a gun in his hand.

JENNIFER 42

Jennifer's mind was racing as she rushed to the cabin. Where? Where? Where *had* she left that key? The last time she'd had it was the day she'd spent that awful afternoon locked in the cabin with Dr. Rossi, when everyone else had gone ashore at Mykonos. She'd put it in her pocket, of course. What was she wearing?

She knew she was puffing, making noise running, and people she passed on the stairs looked startled as they looked back at whoever was behind them, wondering what the noise was, but Jennifer didn't care. She remembered now. The navy shorts that had to be ironed just so, which was why she hardly ever wore them. She skidded to a halt in front of the door and fumbled for the key to her own cabin, flung open the door and began scrambling through the tangle of clothes in her bottom drawer. Thank goodness most of her clothes were white or summery colours, the navy showed up and was easy to find, and yes, the key was in the pocket. She didn't even try to close the drawer, just rushed out of the cabin slamming the door behind her. Let Dr. Rossi try to figure *that* out when he listened to the tape of what went on in their cabin.

There was nobody in the passageway on Sam's deck when she got there. She slowed down as she neared the cabin, trying to control her breathing. The puffing would be a dead giveaway. She should have thought of that sooner and paced herself better. Still, she decided, it wouldn't hurt to listen for a minute before she opened the door, it might give her an idea of what was going on. She needed some kind of plan of action.

She could hear Dr. Rossi's voice, it sounded insistent, but she couldn't make out the words and Sam wasn't saying much. All she could think of, now that her breathing was back to normal, was getting into the room and – and what? She realized now that, if worse came to worst, she hadn't brought anything to hit Rossi with, and if she had, it would show when she went into the cabin. She just had to hope that when she got inside she could find something, a shoe or something, if she needed to.

"No!" Sam's voice was protesting loud enough that she could make it out.

Move it Jennifer, she thought. She stuck the key in the lock, turned it and flung the door open, at the same time dropping to the floor. She could see Rossi spin around, the gun in his hand, one arm in a hammerlock on Sam's neck, but it was all a blur as she rolled in and squeezed herself as tightly as she could between the beds, out of his way. Rossi stared out into the hallway for a second then kicked the door shut with his foot.

"What the hell...!" The gun was at Sam's head now. "What's going on here?" His voice was icy cold. "You kids have made contact with Arnold, haven't you?" His arm tightened on Sam's throat. "Where is he?"

Now, thought Jennifer, but she was miles from anything that might be used as a weapon. Sam's notebook was useless, so were the paperback books on the shelf by the bed. She stood up. Nothing to do but climb on the bed and jump on Dr. Rossi from behind, maybe the surprise would be enough to make him let go so Sam could get away. Execpt...except.... She hesitated. He'd probably shoot Sam first. Sam was making strangling noises. She had to do something, but what?

Then she heard the key turning in the lock and relief swept over her. Rossi hadn't noticed she'd left it sticking in the door. The door swung open and Brady jumped out of sight just as Rossi fired. There was no report, just a gasping sound from the gun and Jennifer realized that the funny-looking extension on the barrel must be a silencer. She hoped Grand and Maggie were well out of the way.

Brady didn't fire back, just poked his gun around the corner. Just then another voice spoke. Jennifer recognized it as belonging to the big woman with the dirty white runners.

"You needn't think you can get rid of another agent, like you did Stavros," she said coldly.

That was all very well, thought Jennifer, but Rossi was holding Sam like a shield. She realized he could hold Brady and the woman at bay and use Sam as a hostage, maybe even get away. It was up to her.

It was then that she noticed that the drawers of the bedside table were ajar. She remembered that Dr. Rossi's held that computer thing. Not very big, but if she threw it... She pulled open the drawer as quietly as she could. There was no little computer but, even better, there was a gun. If she moved quietly and quickly and stood on the bed she could bring it down on Rossi's head hard enough to knock him out. Hardly daring to breathe, she picked it up and moved around behind Rossi.

Jennifer hadn't bargained for the fact that Brady would be seeing a gun floating through the air behind Rossi. His expression of horror was better than any old "look behind you" trick. It was enough to tip Rossi off that there was something going on behind him. Rossi spun around before Jennifer had a chance to get close enough to hit him. She got ready to throw the gun. It seemed her only chance.

She had to hand it to Brady, even in a state of shock the man was fast. Fast and strong. He was through the door and had grabbed Rossi's gun arm and twisted it pulling the gun away from Sam's head. The woman was inside now and slammed her gun down on Rossi's temple so that he crumpled to the floor, releasing Sam – who looked about ready to do some crumpling of his own, but managed just to sit on the foot of his bed rubbing his throat.

The gun Jennifer'd found lay innocently on the bed, and she was back huddled on the floor against the bedside table, a position she'd assumed when she realized that Brady and the woman had things under control and she'd be wise to duck, in case there was any shooting.

"Mrs. Arnold," Brady called. "It's alright, but you'd better check on your young friend." He was staring at the gun lying on the bed, but he didn't say anything.

Grand and Maggie came rushing around the corner into the room.

"Oh Sam!" Maggie was sitting beside him, all sympathy. "Are you alright?"

Jennifer resisted the urge to give her a good swift kick.

Maggie was the only one on deck the next morning when the launch pulled up to the side of the ship. She'd come up just after sunrise to lie on a deck chair and read in peace, but mostly she'd come to get away from Jennifer.

"Too much excitement yesterday," Grand had said, looking concerned.

Maybe so, Maggie thought, but when Jennifer was restless she was impossible to sleep with. *She* slept, but Maggie had finally given up and decided that a deck chair all to herself would be preferable to being kicked and elbowed for another minute.

She'd been standing at the rail, just watching the seabirds and wondering if the bit of land she could see was part of Turkey or just another Greek islet. She had her little binoculars around her neck and was trying to check it out, when she realized there was something happening below her.

What looked like a us Navy launch had come alongside the ship at the place the tender boats picked up passengers to go ashore, at those islands where the ship couldn't dock. Almost automatically she focused her binoculars on it to watch. Three people got on board the launch. She recognized them instantly. First the woman agent – Christa, was the name Brady'd used for her – then Dr. Rossi, and then Brady himself. They'd gone in the cabin of the boat and then Brady had come quickly back out and jumped back on the ship and disappeared as the launch pulled away. It had all taken less than two minutes. She looked down at the rails of the decks below. Anyone watching would have had to lean over the rail as she was doing, and she saw no one. She was probably the only passenger who'd noticed a thing.

So Rossi, or whoever the man really was, was gone. She wondered if there would be a big CIA double-agent scandal back in the States. Jennifer had concocted a cloak-and-dagger theory that there wouldn't be. Jen had hung around with Brady and Christa while they were waiting for Rossi to come to, and she was convinced that they were going to take him to Crete where he would conveniently "disappear." Something to do with Stavros' family providing "hospitality."

Maggie wasn't much concerned. Last night she'd been more worried about Sam. He'd spent the night in the ship's sick bay. He couldn't talk yet except for a kind of croaking sound, so they'd written notes back and forth, and Maggie had read to him just to keep him company.

Jennifer came to visit too, but she'd just made fun of the croaking saying, "Nevermore! Nevermore!" every time Sam tried to say anything. She said she'd just come for a laugh anyway, and it was a good thing nobody was around when she finally did and began to reappear.

Sometimes, Maggie thought settling herself on the deck chair, Jennifer can be amazingly unsympathetic.

It seemed to her that she'd only been reading a little while when Grand and Jennifer came to get her for breakfast. Jen plopped herself down on the chair beside Maggie, nearly spilling the suntan lotion, and making Maggie wish she'd stayed asleep. She was about to bawl her out when she noticed that Jennifer was carrying something bulky wrapped in her sweater. Besides, some people were walking by and it might not be wise to draw their attention, with Jennifer you never knew.

"A lovely time of day to be on deck isn't it?" said Grand conversationally, as she sat down on the chair next to Maggie's.

Maggie waited until the people were out of earshot. "Alright," she said, "what's up?"

"Jennifer," Grand explained, "has decided to be sick and not go ashore in Kusadasi today."

"I'm going to hang around the lifeboat and make sure that nothing happens to Dad. We'll be at a Turkish port and if somebody got him and took him ashore..." She looked worried. "I know Mr. Brady seems like a nice man, and he did save Sam yesterday, but I'm glad we didn't tell him we've actually got Dad on board, only that we'd made contact and given him the passports."

Grand nodded, "It's terrible to have to be suspicious of people, isn't it?" She sighed. "I'll feel much better when Rossi is no longer in the vicinity. I half expected Brady to arrange a helicopter to land on the deck before we got inside Turkish jurisdiction."

"He's gone," Maggie said, and told them what she had seen.

"I wonder if they'll really take him to Crete?" Jennifer looked serious. "I'd feel sorrier for him if he hadn't double-crossed poor Stavros."

"I doubt that will happen, Jennifer. More likely the American authorities will try to exchange him for the real Dr. Rossi. Poor man, I hope his captors haven't decided he was expendable in the meantime. I'm afraid those are the risks in the Secret Agent job description." Grand looked at Jennifer sternly. "I want you to keep that in mind young lady, and not go getting any silly ideas for the future."

Jennifer laughed, "No, Grand. A nice quiet detective agency will suit me fine." She let go of her sweater bundle and it fell with a heavy thud near Maggie's foot.

"Ouch! Jennifer! What the...?"

Jennifer opened the sweater and showed Maggie. "It's a dumbbell. I borrowed it from the weight room in the ship's gym. It's going to go invisible when I do." Maggie looked incredulous. "I'm tired of not having anything handy to bash people on the head with," Jennifer explained, "if anybody threatens Dad while you guys are ashore...Pow!" She swung her arm menacingly.

Grand looked concerned. "Jennifer, I'd be the last person to say that you rescuing Maggie and being crucial in saving Sam was anything but wonderful, but I do hope you will be able to drop the habit of 'bashing people on the head' once this trip is over. It just isn't nice, Dear."

"Sure Grand," Jennifer laughed and got up. "Do we call for Sam on the way to breakfast? They'll probably serve him gruel or pablum or something if he stays in the infirmary."

"The doctor did say he would be fine to leave this morning and to go ashore with us." Grand stood up and began to follow her. "I think it would be good for him to go, it will take his mind off what happened yesterday."

"Can't wait to see old Gamgee...we can have a nice talk...Nevermore... Nevermore..." Jennifer croaked as she hopped down the stairs.

There were six of them sitting around the table at the rooftop restaurant in Athens less than a week later. Everybody was beaming.

Jennifer especially. Today her dad had finally been able to leave the Canadian Embassy. There would be more debriefing when he got back to Canada via Washington. A lot of people wanted to ask him questions about the events that led up to his imprisonment in Syria and, Sam was sure, there'd be a lot of questions about the man posing as Dr. Anthony Rossi. But Mr. Arnold had been allowed to meet them for their last night in Greece. And Jennifer had been able to hug her dad at last.

Getting James Arnold safely off the ship in Rhodes and knowing he'd arrived safely at the Embassy in Athens had been great. But Sam's happiest moment had already happened by then. It had been when they went ashore in Kusadasi and he saw his Grandfather waiting for him on the dock.

Sam smiled across at him now and decided that was about as good as it gets. Grandad hadn't ignored the things

Sam had said on the phone. He'd flown to Turkey to come to Sam's rescue.

"You can imagine my feelings when I realized that there was something very strange going on and Sam was somehow stuck in the midst of it," he was saying to Grandmother Arnold.

Sam grinned at Jennifer. She wasn't the only one who had a terrific grandparent. The last three days of the trip had been a dream come true, as far as Sam was concerned. And it was nice that the grandparents seemed to get along so well. They both were great travellers and Grand seemed to know a surprising amount about archaeology.

The first night back in his old cabin without Dr. Rossi might have been upsetting after the time he'd spent the day before fearing for his life; instead he was sharing the cabin with Grandad, who'd managed to book passage for the last few days of the cruise. Couldn't be better, he thought again.

"We managed to piece together what must have happened to the real Tony Rossi. He was studying some excavations in Turkey...at Bogazkoy, the ancient Hittite capital...when the switch was made," Grandad was explaining. "I suppose he would just have disappeared if his imposter had succeeded in capturing you, James."

The girls' father nodded. He had done very little talking during the meal, eating his lamb souvlaki while feasting his eyes on his two daughters. He still looked thin and pale, but his face didn't seem so sallow now that he was looking relaxed and happy. "I'm sure he would never have gone to the States. Even if he got a position at a different University, it would only have been a matter of time before someone recognized that he was not Anthony Rossi. If I hadn't ended up in prison with the real Professor Rossi, it might have been some time before anyone knew what had happened to him."

"It didn't help that the CIA had muddied his trail somewhat," Grandmother Arnold added, "but evidently, at least as far as Brady seems to know, they believed they had the real Tony Rossi too." Grand smiled. "And," she said looking at the girls, "I have a surprise for you two...I talked to your mother this morning and she's agreed to let you come out to Vancouver, as soon as your father gets through the debriefing. Of course, she's looking forward to having you home for a little while first. You can show her some of those pictures Sam's taken."

"So," said Sam's grandfather as he held up his wine glass to Grand. "A toast to safe travelling!"

Sam smiled as they clinked glasses. He knew Jennifer had been envying him because his holiday would be continuing when he flew to Rome with Grandad next week, now she and Maggie had something to look forward to, too.

Jennifer waved her glass in the air. "Waiter! Bring on the champagne!" She did a pratfall off her chair.

Everyone laughed except Maggie, who looked disgusted. "Jennifer! People will think that isn't just Coke in that glass."

Jennifer climbed back onto her chair. "Another toast!" She picked up her water goblet. "To Arnold and Elwin, Detectives!"

"Elwin and..." Sam began but Maggie interrupted.

"Make that *Arnold,* Elwin and Arnold!" She said clinking her glass with Sam.

Jennifer looked surprised. "Okay," she said, "I'll drink to that!"

Sam was amazed. Jennifer wasn't arguing. Surely she

realized what Maggie meant. But then, he decided, maybe Jennifer was caught up in the happiness of the moment. He looked over at the Acropolis above them. Great.

Grandad held out his glass to Grand. "A toast to grand-children!"

"Grandchildren and Greece," she smiled.

James Arnold lifted his glass to all of them. "And happy endings!" he said.

Everyone clinked their glasses. "I've got to get a picture of this," Sam grabbed his camera. Probably won't need a flash, he thought – there was enough light from their smiles.

ACKNOWLEDGEMENTS

The author wishes to thank Geoffrey Ursell and all the wonderful people at Coteau books who decided to publish this improved and updated edition as the first in The Spy Who Wasn't There series. And as always thanks to my husband Earl Georgas who is an amazing proofreader – among other things!

photo: Benje Bondar

Cora Taylor is one of Canada's best-known children's authors, having published more than a dozen juvenile novels, including the *Ghost Voyages* trilogy and *The Deadly Dance* for Coteau. Other recent titles include *On Wings of a Dragon,* and *Angelique – The Buffalo Hunt.*

Her books have won many awards, including the Canada Council Children's Literature Prize, the Canadian Library Association's Book of the Year Award, the Ruth Schwartz Book Award, and Alberta's R. Ross Annett Award for Children's Literature.

Cora Taylor was born and raised in Saskatchewan, moved to Edmonton in the 1950s, and studied writing with the likes of Rudy Wiebe and W.O. Mitchell. She currently divides her time between Edmonton, Ontario, and Florida.

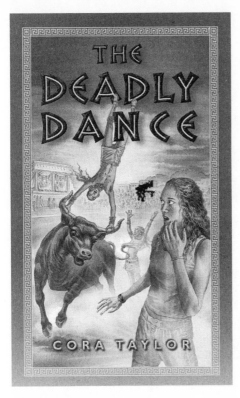